The Adventures of Tinguely Querer

For Worth,
I hope you enjoy the read —
thank you for everything! — (!)
this is a "big print" edition — (!)
let me know if you'd
like the "normal" print, too ☺
with appreciation
and admiration —
Susan
May 16, 2011

The Adventures of Jinguely Querer

SUSAN SMITH NASH

Acknowledgements

Thank you to the editors of the following magazines in which Tinguely Querer's adventures orginally appeared:

Big Bridge: "Arroyo"; "Big Big Sky"; "Crystal Skull"
Gargoyle: "Panhandle Coin and Gun Shop"
Press 1: "Air-Clipping with Zoroaster: The Sun-Magnolia Refinery"; "Illusion of Time"; "The Wildcatters"

A joint publication between

VODNIKOVA ZALOŽBA (DSKG)
Editor: Jana Bauer
Suhadolčanova 64
1000 Ljubljana, Slovenia

TEXTURE PRESS
1108 Westbrooke Terrace
Norman, OK 73072
U.S.A.

For ordering information,
please visit the Texture Press website at
www.texturepress.org.

ISBN: 978-0-9797573-9-6

Cover art: *Circlus* by Denise Scicluna
www.denisescicluna.com

Interior drawings by Susan Smith Nash

Book design by Arlene Ang

Table of Contents

Stuck on a West Texas pipeline project, Tinguely Querer found herself having to share an office with a parrot named LouLou who had nothing better to do all day than to squawk lines from Flaubert in Québécois-accented French.

"Félicité! Félicité!" squawked the parrot.

"Hello! Goodbye! Hello! Buenos días!" squawked Tinguely, in an attempt to expand the parrot's vocabulary.

Tinguely did not know which was more unbearable: the parrot or a woman she met at the motel pool. The woman, who was a political strategist, swam every evening. She was a strong swimmer, knifing through the water with smooth, powerful strokes.

The motel had put in a regulation indoor pool because they could rent out lanes to the local swim club, which used it for practice and also for time trials. Motel guests could use the lanes as well. With a five-foot-high pace clock on each end, the pool was perfect for working out.

"Hi. My name is Coeur Flandelle," she said when she first introduced herself at the side of the pool. Her blonde hair was drying in shiny, chlorine-damaged clumps. "I'm doing pre-publicity for the rally to announce that Senator Blixen has secured a $6.5 million earmark for a project here in West Texas."

"Coors like the beer?" asked Tinguely.

"No," said the woman. Tinguely thought she heard her mutter "idiot" under her breath, but it wasn't clear. The children swimming in the pool were splashing.

"Coeur, like Coeur d'Alene," she continued.

"I'm Tinguely Querer, and I'm working on a project," explained Tinguely. She pronounced her name "TAN glee" as would the Swiss.

She did not explain that the pipeline project also involved

developing a security plan for above-ground pipelines in Venezuela, Ecuador, Colombia, Nigeria, and for the Baku-Ceyhan pipeline covering Azerbaijan, Georgia, and Turkey (circumventing Armenia and Russia, much to the displeasure of each). She did not like the project much.

In Tinguely's opinion, it was impossible to provide any reasonable security, apart from ongoing campaign contributions to national, regional and local officials, and overpaid employment of prominent townspeople in villages bordering the pipeline. Nevertheless, she was willing to try. She secretly hoped the company she was doing consulting for would not actually try to implement a plan. She did not want to think that her ideas might be responsible for bloodshed or generalized chaos. Her general approach was to introduce chaos into the local thuggery and a soaring sense of self-interest and self-preservation into the elites.

"Nice to meet you, Tingly," said Coeur. She mispronounced Tinguely's name.

****

Tinguely was 30. It was an awkward age, and she did not like it at all. It offered no benefits as far as Tinguely was concerned. No respect. No youth.

Sometimes, when the sunlight caught her hair a certain way and her face lost the pensive cast it usually had, she looked 25.

At other times, after long drives, conversations with clients, or disconcerting encounters, she retreated back into herself. It was always a response to invasive energy.

At those times, it was always the same. Her face was a mask. Her posture was formal and tense. At those times, despite her soft lips and warm eyes, she seemed 35, even 38.

year of
the CLONe

utopia,
inc.

****

LouLou was starting to develop an attachment to Tinguely. Perhaps it was the other way around.

After all, Tinguely did spend a lot of time on the road and, other than long conversations with her dad, who always managed to irritate her because he made her feel guilty, she had no one to talk to.

LouLou always squawked the same thing when Tinguely walked into the office.

"Félicité! Félicité!" That always made Tinguely smile. Félicité could be either a woman's name or a shout of happiness.

"I'm happy, too, LouLou!" Tinguely said. Then she took out a cupful of LouLou's favorite "Tropical Parrot Mix" and poured some into the bowl. Then she hand-fed LouLou almonds. LouLou would cock her head, open her beak and, with her tongue, gently take it from Tinguely's finger. Tinguely loved watching how LouLou skillfully and neatly cracked the shell, extracted the nutmeat, and then ate it.

One day she brought LouLou a packet of dried cherries from a cherry festival held each year in northern Michigan. Another day she brought her golden raisins imported from Jordan. Another day it was organic Calimyrna figs.

LouLou squawked and trilled happily at the new treats.

After feeding her, Tinguely would take her out of her cage, place her on her shoulder, and bring a small perch to the office with her files, maps, computer, fax/scanner/copier, and digitizer table. It was oddly comforting to have LouLou in the room as Tinguely pored over maps, statistics and reports.

"You're great, LouLou. You keep me from getting a headache."

"Félicité! Félicité!"

****

"What most politicians forget is that there is no real way to protect themselves. So, you just have to preemptively exploit vulnerabilities," said Coeur. Tinguely was panting on the side of the pool after having tried to keep up with Coeur's long, lean, powerful strokes. It had been a tactical error. Now she was too breathless to change the subject.

"Oh?" Tinguely tried to regulate her breathing to seem more in shape.

"Everyone's one big, exposed nerve," Coeur said. She paused. "No. It's more like an exposed aorta. Imagine if you wore your aorta on the surface of your skin."

"Everyone would wear armor," said Tinguely.

"Yes and no. Armor for the illusion of protection. No way to shield it, really. So, everyone walks around knowing the other is just waiting for the vulnerable moment. Eventually their time will come though. Someone will cut the artery."

"Sounds messy," said Tinguely.

"Yes. And it's just a matter of time. And everyone will see it," said Coeur. She glanced at Tinguely.

"Ready for another set?" she asked. "Five one hundreds on the 1:30? Or 1:45?"

Tinguely took the bait.

"1:30 sounds good."

She regretted it.

****

Then she went on to explain that she was planning to stay a few extra days. With a conspiratorial inclination of the head, she leaned toward Tinguely and spoke in a low voice.

"I want to meet Father LaFavre," she said. Father LaFavre was the founder of a church centered on healing. The word was, it was very hands-on.

"Sexual healing?" asked Tinguely. "Why would you need that?"

"Something, but I'm not sure," said Coeur. "I can describe the symptoms if you'd like."

"No. That's okay." Tinguely had no interest in knowing more. She preferred to think of political strategists as being vaguely non-corporeal, except for the occasional subterranean revelations that might appear in blogs and tabloids. A political strategist with dry skin who smelled of chlorine was good for sharing insights into Machiavelli, but that was about it, in Tinguely's estimation.

"By the looks of you, you need it more than I," Coeur said. "Prudish? Or maybe just hypocritical."

"I'm a pragmatist, Cur," said Tingly, sweetly. She then took off her swim goggles and looked off into the distance. A confrontation with a person who had made a career of orchestrating social chaos and political ruin did not appeal to her. "You think hooking up with the healer will help? If you don't mind, what do need to have healed?"

"Stress. Politicians who will not follow their handlers. People who just can't be trusted to follow logic or common sense," Coeur sighed loudly. She scratched her arm, then the side of her belly. Tinguely decided Coeur was suffering from a bad case of itchy, flaky, dry skin.

"Have you tried moisturizer?" asked Tinguely. The strategist had a way of tunelessly humming Gregorian chants when she did not want to participate further in the conversation. Tinguely wondered if she had picked up that habit at the convent, or if she had developed it while driving across country, listening to Gregorian chants on CD in her hail-damaged Pathfinder.

"He must touch me, and then I will touch him. We will

cleave," she hummed tunelessly.

"And that will make you cloven," said Tinguely, under her breath. "As in hooves."

"What? What did you say?" said Coeur, startled.

"Was that Senator Blixen's campaign anthem?" asked Tinguely, in her most polite voice.

"I am going to find out what it is that makes him so special. I am getting some healing. I am getting a lot. No one can stop me." Coeur's eyes glinted. The whites of her eyes, bright red from the chlorine, contrasted with her light gray irises. Her face was momentarily a small gargoyle drainspout on the side of a French cathedral.

"Ew," said Tinguely to herself. "Just ew. And ick."

Tinguely fought the impulse to push the political strategist into the pool and steal her flip-flops, glasses and towel. Such aggression would be pointless, she told herself. She looked over at Coeur, whose face had reverted back to its golden fulsomeness. As usual, she was looking disconcertingly pure and perky, and not at all capable of insinuating that a war hero had ratted out his buddies, or a family man toe-tapped in airport bathrooms known for anonymous sexual encounters. Perhaps she could slip a purgative into the woman's green tea frappucino.

"Your back is peeling," Tinguely said. "Looks like alligator skin."

Coeur smiled sweetly at Tinguely.

"You seem to have hair on your chest. You might check your testosterone levels." Coeur paused. "Oh. And tell them to cut off the nut bag. It's not attractive on you."

If anyone would end up drinking a purgative slipped into her specialty coffeehouse drink, it would be Tinguely. Coeur had effectively turned the tables. She was good. Tinguely had to give her that.

****

It had been a rough night. Tinguely was wracked by nightmares that she could not remember when she awoke except to feel that she had been visited by an incubus.

The waking effect was not as pleasant as one might hope a secret, furtive, unconscious sexual encounter might be. But then, violation is never the thrill popular culture tries to pretend it is.

The day was already hot, but the office was cool. The smell of brewing coffee cheered Tinguely. She sipped a cup as she turned on her computer and scanned the website of the New York Times. Her reverie was interrupted by a terrible squawk.

« – Mon Dieu ! comme vous êtes bête !! »

"What??? What are you saying??" asked Tinguely. It was LouLou, the lovely parrot of green, blue and gold feathers, and a bright orange beak. "Polly Want A Cracker?"

Tinguely had a intrusive thought. Shreds of the dream she had flashed into her consciousness. It made her long for the man who would be the love of her life, whom she had yet to meet.

"Mon Dieu!" squawked LouLou. "My God! You're such a beast!"

Tinguely sighed. The parrot also recited parts of the Mass, also in French. But he always returned back to Flaubert:

« Félicité ! la porte, la porte ! »

"Can you recite anything from Madame Bovary?" asked Tinguely. "If you did, I'd bring you straightaway to my friend, the former nun. She needs to know what this seduction business can do to her."

« Félicité ! la porte, la porte ! » Apparently the Flaubert that LouLou knew was from Flaubert's widely anthologized short story *Un coeur simple* ("A Simple Heart").

The door opened. A man who looked like a venture capitalist or a televangelist walked in.

"Is this the Calgon Hills MegaChurch office?" he asked. "I'm here to check on the arrangements—I think I'm supposed to be at the Calgon Hills church, or at the football stadium. The details they sent were sketchy."

"This is Calgon Hills, but I don't live here. I'm just working on a project for a week," said Tinguely. "The pipeline."

« – Mon Dieu ! comme vous êtes bête !! » squawked LouLou. "You're such a beast!"

"Your parrot speaks French," said the man.

"Yes." Long pause. "What's your name?"

"Father LaFavre."

« – Mon Dieu ! comme vous êtes bête !! » LouLou and Tinguely squawked in unison.

****

"I should have a set of maps and a strategic plan for you by next Wednesday," said Tinguely to her client. She took the Bluetooth out of her ear and looked at it skeptically. Her head always felt as though it were vibrating after she used it for any length of time. Brain tumors. Just what she needed.

Things were not going well in the office. She was reviewing West Texas pipeline's corrosion control plan. At the same time, she was trying to wrap up the plan to provide security for an aboveground, highly strategic pipeline, but she despaired of ever coming up with a plan that would work. Pipelines were just too vulnerable, especially those that had been designed to be above-ground. They were open invitations to all those who were curious about the best way to disrupt the economy or political stability.

It had been determined that a single gunshot from a high-caliber sniper rifle could cause an explosion and spill.

It had also been determined that a single grass fire around the pipeline would heat up the contents enough to create an explosion.

A collision with a bulldozer, tractor, or backhoe would be equally calamitous.

****

"Are you sure you want to meet Father LaFavre?" asked Tinguely. Coeur looked at her curiously.

"Absolutely. Now more than ever," Coeur said. She toweled her long golden hair and shoved her arms into a large terrycloth robe, identical to those used by the Olympic team. Her arms and legs were a gorgeous shade of gold. Tinguely looked down at her own, still flushed and pink from exertion.

"It seems futile to me. What a charlatan," she said.

"How do you know?" asked Coeur.

"I don't know. I'm just looking at probability and statistics," said Tinguely.

"What happened to faith?" asked Coeur.

"It's all about performance. Can he do it? Really heal? Or just con people really well?" said Tinguely.

"I have my own reasons. That's all I have to say. But, well—Tinguely—it's something I want more than anything I have ever wanted in my entire life," she said, actually pronouncing Tinguely's name correctly.

Tinguely was shocked in spite of herself. She had never imagined someone so profoundly cynical, Machiavellian, even Rasputin-like, would have such a capacity for suspension of disbelief. She seemed to truly believe in the appearance of things; in profound innocence and goodness.

It made Tinguely a bit sad. Coeur adjusted her thick terry

robe, and Tinguely thought of the race horse, Filly Eight Belles, who broke her legs as she came in second at the Kentucky Derby. Her jockey whipped her and made her run despite stress fractures.

Filly Eight Belles was destroyed right there on the track in front of the crowd, even before they could take her off, before anyone could even examine her injuries. She was taken out with a single, clean shot.

It was all about performance.

****

Tinguely noticed that not all of Coeur's Rove-ian machinations worked as well as hoped. Senator Blixen had secured a $6.5 million earmark to pave the way for massive wind turbine farms in the county. It would bring millions of dollars of revenues to small, drought-stricken West Texas towns.

It would bring employment to construction crews. There would be a surplus of electricity to sell. Plus, an internet provider was piggybacking and creating extensive Wi-Fi networks.

Nevertheless, someone had organized protesters who held posters complaining about the noise, the electric fields, even the shadows cast by the arms of the wind turbines.

Someone had organized protesters holding nicely lettered banners and placards:

MY COWS DON'T NEED ELECTROSHOCK THERAPY

ELECTROMAGNETIC FIELDS KILL

WIND • NOISE

Tinguely thought the complaint was a bit ridiculous. She thought of the Joni Mitchell song lyrics—something about paving paradise into a parking lot.

How did the anti-energy people plan to live? If they were against green energy, what hope was there for them?

She suspected the protest was organized by Senator Blixen's political rivals and/or rival energy companies unable to get the leases and right-of-ways.

"Coeur, tell me. I've always wondered. Does it do any good to go public with the hidden agendas?" Tinguely asked Coeur as they rinsed off under the poolside shower and put on their swim caps and goggles in anticipation of their evening swim.

"Not really. You just end up emphasizing the parts of the story you don't want people to think about. Better to use distraction and diversionary tactics."

****

"Your church invented sexual healing, right? Weren't you accused of operating a brothel without a license?"

Father LaFavre looked at her sternly. Tinguely couldn't believe she had squawked out the words. While Tinguely spoke, LouLou whistled and did low trills.

Then he smiled, "The tabloids love that stuff. No one serious about finding out about us believed that. It's metaphorical, but it is powerful."

Tinguely sighed.

"People have imaginations," he said.

Tinguely was disappointed.

****

Tinguely realized that Coeur was running late for the rally. It was not actually a rally, but a church service, but Tinguely did not see that there was really any difference at all. Coeur might have agreed with her, if she had known what she thought.

Tinguely knew she could have given Coeur a ride to the event, but she did not want to have to wait around after the service if Coeur really did intend to follow up on her foolish desire to seduce a man of the cloth. Perhaps Father LaFavre was not a man of cut from ordinary religious fabric, but there were deities in the mix. It was not good to play games with one's higher power. Like the Israelites in the Old Testament, Tinguely would not utter the name of her higher power. It was forbidden.

However, Tinguely was surrounded by people who used the name of their higher power loosely, name-droppingly, even manically, as though they had a mild form of Tourette's syndrome.

The event was billed as a Special Healing Revival, and Father LaFavre would be in the pulpit and on the "Healing Platform" for three nights in a row. Her commitments with the Senator forced her to miss the first two, but there was nothing that would keep her from attending the last one.

It was just as well that Tinguely was not going to give Coeur a ride to the revival. LouLou suddenly suffered an attack of horrendous separation anxiety and would not let Tinguely leave the office. Even after covering the cage with a blanket, LouLou continued to squawk so loudly one could hear it from the street.

Having no other option, Tinguely packed LouLou into her traveling cage and placed her in the back seat. Although one might not expect to see a bird at a healing session, it would probably be acceptable. After all, the music was loud, people would be shouting, perhaps even speaking in tongues.

"Félicité! Félicité!" squawked LouLou as they hit a bump.

« – Mon Dieu ! comme vous êtes bête !! » snapped back Tinguely. She could quote Flaubert as well as any parrot.

Tinguely sighed. It was going to be a long night.

As she wondered how and why precisely she felt so compelled to go to a rally she did not wholly endorse, Tinguely reflected upon Coeur's quest. A flash thought entered her mind. She envisioned Coeur poking her fingers into LouLou's cage, and LouLou severing the index finger at the knuckle, with a clean clip of her beak. Flesh and bone were a lot softer than almond shells, after all.

Tinguely smiled at the thought of LouLou spitting out a severed finger. Feeling guilty and fearful of reprisals for such violent thoughts, Tinguely prayed a quick prayer of forgiveness.

****

"Come forth, all those who seek to be HEALED!"

The organ blared, and the church guitars and drums kicked in. It was an amazing rush. The lights dimmed, people in the audience started to move, chant, speak in tongues, sway back and forth.

The lights were purple black, and every other person held a light stick, the kind one might have seen at a rave in the late 90s. The scent of almond, pumpkin spice, and iced coffee wafted through. There was a coffee bar at the entrance, and people were still coming in with pumpkin spice lattes, the evening's specialty.

"Heal! Heal! HEALING!! It is YOURS!!" Father LaFavre was dressed in what appeared to be a dark Nehru jacket and long pants with purple, rose, and lemon neon piping.

"Is that Paul Oakenfold? Armin van Buuren? Ministry of Sound? The Thrillseekers?" Tinguely was astonished. They were playing her favorite techno DJs. A track from one of her favorite Hed Kandi compilations came across the sound system, accompanied by organ and drums, live on stage.

"Wow." Tinguely was speechless. She loved it. Her body started swaying spontaneously with the pulsing beat. Next to her, a woman wearing a long flowing dress and strings of beads looped on her arms as bracelets was chanting Nam Miyoho Rengi Ko. Others were chanting the Lord's Prayer, others were chanting Psalms 23. It was a free-for-all chant to rave music.

A woman made hula moves with her arms, a deep beaming joyous smile on her face. She was making her way to the front to the Healing Platform. With a start, Tinguely realized it was Coeur.

LouLou was uncharacteristically quiet in her traveling cage. The Hed Kandi's remix of Audio-Fraud's "Music to Me" came on.

"Félicité! Félicité!" squawked LouLou.

"Yes, yes!" Tinguely tried to watch what was happening on the Healing Platform, but the lights shifted. Distracted by the glowstick, she lost sight of Coeur.

"Heal! Heal! HEALING!! It is YOURS!!" Father LaFavre's voice rang out. Tinguely tried a few hula moves with her arms as "Music to Me" pulsed on.

"Heal! Heal! HEALING!"

****

"What happened to you?" Tinguely and Coeur were at the pool again.

Coeur sported a deep bruise on her left shoulder and bruises that looked like fingerprints on her right forearm.

"I'm not sure. It all happened so fast. I was there, and then I wasn't." Coeur looked disoriented. Tinguely noticed a swelling on her lower lip as well.

"What?" Tinguely was aghast. "Did Father LaFavre do

23

something? I saw you go up, but did not see you after that."

"I don't know. It is a blur. It was a blur."

"Did they give you anything to drink?" asked Tinguely.

"No. No rohypnol, no date rape drug. I was not sexually assaulted." Coeur looked uncharacteristically vulnerable. "But, well, I don't think I received any sort of healing. It's weird. I just became aware of how pathetically weak I was. I still am. I can find the soft places in others, but I just can't seem to pinpoint my own."

"Is self-knowledge a kind of healing?" asked Tinguely.

"I hope not. It never stops bleeding," said Coeur.

"What? What do you mean?" said Tinguely. "Knowledge? Self? The flow of awareness?"

"The human condition, I guess. I don't know. I don't want to know."

After the last workout, they exchanged business cards, email addresses, cell phone numbers. They promised to keep in touch. Tinguely knew they would, even though there would always be an odd rivalry and uncomfortable insight into the subterranean energies of the other.

Veins, aorta, pipelines, transmission lines.

Each one easily taken down by one well-aimed shot.

******

The project had finally come to an end. Tinguely made her presentation via web conference to the clients' remote offices. They logged in from Venezuela, Colombia, Ecuador, Nigeria, Georgia, Algeria, and other places where they needed pipeline security.

"You have to analyze your potential threats, identify their weaknesses. Then, you preemptively strike their vulnerabilities," said Tinguely. Her time with Coeur had not been without benefit.

"How do you do that?"

"Look within yourself first, find out how you're undermining yourself. Then find out who they are using as their advisors," said Tinguely. "It will all be in my final report."

They seemed quite pleased. That gratified Tinguely. After work, she slowly packed her car. The traveling cage with LouLou was the last thing she placed in the passenger side next to her.

They made their way down the highway. Tinguely put on her favorite CD: The Thrillseekers' *Night Music I*, the one with cover art featuring a wind turbine farm. The music soothed and energized her as she reflected back upon the pool, Coeur, and Father LaFavre.

At her side, LouLou squawked contentedly.

"Félicité! Félicité!"

"Absolutely," said Tinguely. The road was long, the stars bright.

A Page from
Tinguely's Journal

The nights are long, and the days are short. I'm getting used to that good old wintertime "besieged" feeling – watching the thieves circle shopping mall parking lots during the holidays.

We realize that when the shopping mall security is highly visible, crime does not stop. It just moves down the street.

The thieves prey upon the sad, hapless marks parked to worship at a church or to play indoor tennis – questioning what it means to worship, to tithe, to pay tribute, to make a sacrifice.

I suppose that you could consider your losses to thieves while you're parked to worship as a kind of involuntary tithing. Imagine if the church officials were in on the game. Honestly, I'd rather not think of that possibility.

Speaking of that "besieged" feeling, why my parents decided to name me Tinguely is beyond comprehension.

It was my mother's idea.

She loved the crazy fountains and self-destructing fountains designed by the 1960s Swiss sculptor, Jean Tinguely.

The name is pronounced "tang-lee," by the way, and not "tingly" or "teengly."

In case you were wondering, it's the French pronunciation.

Passersby walked down the sidewalk in front of the small shop. "Panhandle Coin and Gun" was a clean place, decorated with framed prints of famous gold coins and taxidermied mule deer, pheasants, and two big jackrabbits.

"Where's your jackalope?" asked Tinguely Querer with a smile. The coin dealer laughed.

"A coyote was the best I could do," he said. An entire stuffed coyote was perched on a stand on the western wall. A rubber rattlesnake and a spray of creosote adorned the base of the stand. It should have been garish, but was not.

"Coyotes are good. Tricksters are always good. Jackalopes are better, though," she said. Her hands felt a bit sticky from the SPF 45 skin protection cream she had applied a few moments before. She was trying to protect her skin the best she could.

"That would make quite a trophy," he said. "Pure fantasy, you know."

"Sure. Fantasy is what inspires the hunt in the first place," said Tinguely.

"Let me go into the safe and get what you wanted to see," said the coin dealer. Tinguely nodded. Her gaze shifted automatically to the television screen.

Two talking heads were utterly fascinated by each other's insights into the economy.

"It was a classic boom-bust cycle. Most people get in at the tail-end of the boom. So, there are always a lot of latecomers. They were, of course, the major part of the body count. The latecomers lost big. Greed kills."

"Yes. At that point, there's nothing to do except to get out the pliers. Pull the gold fillings from the corpses."

The program went to commercial break. Tinguely focused on the business at hand. She had been commanded by her father to buy gold. The stock market was firmly in bear territory.

Bonds were weak. Banks were failing.

"Gold. It's the only thing that holds up," her dad said. "It's the best protection."

Tinguely did not agree. Gold was the one thing that pushed people over the edge. It was not liquid. You couldn't eat it. People wanted to steal it. But—she had to do her dad's bidding. She had agreed to it, after all.

The gold coin dealer was explaining the benefits of the new Canadian Maple Leaf .99999 fine gold coins. Tinguely was not paying attention. All she could think of was the image of a financial planner with pliers in his hand, pulling the fillings from his poor chump client who jumped and landed on the sidewalk several floors down from their posh offices.

The talking head on the left side of the screen smiled sweetly.

"Do you remember Drake Management? The San Francisco-based hedge fund? They lost millions of dollars in one week—their hedge funds hurt them. They also had traditional fixed income funds."

The talking head on the right side of the screen looked deeply into the eyes of the left-hand head.

"Oh yes, I do remember that." Sigh. Inhale. Exhale. "It was part of the subprime fueled mortgage debacle."

The coin dealer glanced up at the screen and then looked at Tinguely.

"I don't know why anyone listens to them. Their 'objective' and 'fair' recommendations are just on the things that they've been paid to promote. I call it an infomercial. It's not fair and balanced news reporting. I don't care what they say it is."

"Investing is a science," said one talking head.

"Oh yes," breathed the other. Sigh. Inhale. Exhale.

That was too much for Tinguely. "Investing as a science? Hah! Well, whatever our society calls investing today is not much more than rite, ritual, and mutually gratifying self-delusion. Science seeks truth. Investing is—well—it's a kind of truth, but it's fuzzy. "

"But aren't you a scientist?" asked the coin dealer. "A geologist?"

"In a manner of speaking. But I wish I knew more about the fuzziness we need to build into our models. It's hard to see people suffer," said Tinguely. Her voice was sharp.

"You must have good insights into commodities then," said the coin dealer. His voice was smooth, bland.

"How much are the coins? My dad wants to buy a few," she said. "He is like everyone else. He believes that truth is in the patterns. But where do the patterns come from? If you scratch the surface, they are from someone's prejudices and beliefs."

The coin dealer smiled. "Sounds like you had to read Georges Sorel, too."

Tinguely pictured Sorel sitting on the front bench at a local high-school pep rally, thumping and tapping his cane to the marching band and the cheerleaders shouting and jumping.

Strange bedfellows, indeed.

The coin dealer continued: "I remember Sorel—he said science was 'too much of a conceptual, ideological construction,' and that it crushes our perception of truth through the 'stifling oppression of remorselessly tidy rational organization.'"

Sorel said systems always were simply skin, stretched tight over belief, faith, and ideology.

Tinguely smiled politely.

"How much are they? My dad's expecting me to haggle with you a bit. Do you mind?" she asked.

The talking heads were still talking, still reinforcing each other's prejudices and each other's rationalizations of the consequences of untrammeled greed.

The coins glittered in the morning light. The voices on the television droned on about predictive models and the science of supply and demand. The multiple working hypotheses were simply variants of dogma.

Frankly, she did not care. She was more interested in tales of the survivors of boom-bust cycles.

The dead coyote smiled. Its canine tooth glinted, the eyes shone dark and black as though to tell her not to bother, not to forget it had been felled by a brass-casinged hollow-point bullet that glittered like gold. Survivors? There weren't any.

Ask any investor.

My dad's last name is Querer.

What kind of last name is that? In Spanish, "querer" means to want or to love.

My dad says it's a Scottish name, Kerr, but that one of his ancestors believed that there were too many Kerrs in the area, and he felt he was truly special – not at all like the bland, stolid Kerrs in his district.

His first choice was to change the spelling to Cur. But it had unfortunate additional meanings – one of which (a badly behaved dog of indifferent parentage) was already thought to reflect his character.

So, he went from Kerr to Querer, landing only briefly on Cur – but it was enough to soak up some of the attributes, namely that of being a compulsive barker.

Consequently, over the years, I've tried to muzzle myself.

I've largely failed.

Tinguely Querer decided to take a few weeks off between contracts and to play the stock market. Granted, it was in the middle of a bear market of historic proportions, but that did not deter Tinguely.

Her last contract had been to buy mineral interests for elderly people in the Texas Panhandle. Most lived in nursing homes and appreciated the help. She had been working out of Caprock, Texas, situated between two large wind turbine farms and a feedlot.

Having signed a short-term rental agreement on a house in the town's newest subdivision, Tinguely decided to stay. It was convenient, and she would be comfortable as she figured out how to profit from panic selling, fear, and raging bears. Plugging in her laptop and G3 card, Tinguely could get high-speed Internet and follow the market, even in the most barren patches of the High Plains.

"All the big money was made during bear markets," said someone on the radio.

Tinguely supposed one could say that about the Great Plague of 1665 (i.e. the Black Death) and the 2004 Boxing Day Tsunami as well. Someone pries the molars and the gold fillings from skulls and, with a little bit of pluck, starts a jewelry shop. When life hands you lemons … get a pair of pliers.

It was a stretch. Tinguely would be the first to admit she knew little or nothing about analyzing market trends and selecting stocks. The work she was doing for her dad and other clients had to do with oil and gas leasing and environmental evaluations. As the business soared, Tinguely started to feel a firm sense of identity.

Her dad, on the other hand, saw the other side. His friends and old business partners had been gutted by margin calls. Some lost up to two billion dollars of net worth in a single day. Now, the companies they had worked so hard to build and own a stake in would suddenly change. Instead of being a major stockholder, Dad's friends would be onlookers. The vultures would be in the driver's seat. Tinguely could tell it bothered Dad.

"Watch yourself, Tinguely. Don't get too cocky. You haven't seen what I've seen. You're young. I'm not," he said.

Tinguely listened, but the words did not register. His experience was not hers.

"I don't feel sorry for them. In fact, I'm glad I did not own stock in their companies. They were narcissistic. When they bought shares in their own companies using borrowed money, what did that really mean, Dad? They hoped to profiteer on insider information. Instead, they devastated lots of people's portfolios," she said.

"Easy to gloat until it happens to you."

"I'm planning to build shareholder value." Tinguely's personal boom had made her bold. She could invent herself. After all, she had already done it successfully.

Constructing an identity was on her mind. Now was the time to come up with a company name, or at least a concept name for the types of services she provided.

A bold name for a newly bold woman. The idea made Tinguely laugh. She knew, in her heart of hearts, she had been feeling vulnerable and unsettled since turning 30 a few months ago.

"By the way, Tinguely, can you meet with our client in Amarillo tomorrow?"

"Sure," said Tinguely.

****

The drive from Caprock to Amarillo was long and dull, but

24-7 talk radio made it bearable.

FOX NEWS, FAIR AND BALANCED: The market took another apocalyptic plunge today, the Dow sinking 500 points while the President was giving a pep talk about the economy. Rumors are out there that when the derivative hedges come due, the market will really dive, since derivatives represent—if you believe what the experts are saying—16 times the world's GDP. More than one person has already said it. When the derivatives tank, the Illuminati will take off their masks, and the Reptilian Aliens, who have been controlling the Illuminati (and the Freemasons) for the last three centuries, will take over.

On the other hand, perhaps Armageddon isn't just around the corner after all. In the last hour of trading, the market soared and the Dow closed 400 points up.

****

> Climbing vines, creepers—
> Our steel fences are overwrought:
> gold melts, money burns.
>
> (Old Dow Jones haiku, with kireji)

****

The only trouble with her plan was she could not sleep. Between LouLou, her large, noisy parrot, and the next door neighbor's incessantly barking pugs, Tinguely was a wreck. Yet again, it was 3 a.m. and she was nowhere near being able to sleep. Neither was LouLou.

Play the ponies.

It was an unwelcome intrusive thought. It made no sense. There weren't any ponies around. Besides, Tinguely didn't like the idea of horse-racing. Never trust a horse. It knows it can be shot if it breaks a leg.

****

Tinguely met her neighbor while picking up Diet Coke cans someone had thrown onto the front yard.

Her neighbor, Beryllium Markham, had flown in on her own small plane to check out her investments in the wind farms north and south of town. She was a lean woman with chiseled features, somewhere in her mid-fifties. Her dark hair was pulled back in a chignon. Her stunning eyes were enhanced by eyeliner and lash-thickening mascara, coupled with smooth, flawless skin. She was prosperous and not very approachable.

Holding a copy of the *Wall Street Journal* in one hand, Beryllium smoothed her hair with the other. Beryllium explained that over the last several years, she had been working as a stockbroker who did limited investment banking as well.

"Perhaps you can give me some stock tips," said Tinguely.

"That sounds like a profoundly bad idea," said Beryllium.

Tinguely decided to warm up to her in a different way. She wondered if Beryllium were related to the pioneering female pilot, Beryl Markham.

"Did you ever live in Africa? In Kenya? Fly planes there? Your mom?" asked Tingeley.

"My great aunt. She was Beryl Markham. I'm Beryllium," said the pilot.

"Nice," said Tinguely. But who would name their child Beryllium? Might as well be "Bear." Beryl was a mineral. Beryl occurred in many forms, including emerald and aquamarine. Beryl was beryllium aluminum cyclosilicate. Beryllium was the key element. The attributes of beryllium included extreme heat resistance.

"I think I'd go with being called Beryl. Doesn't sound so … uh … technical."

She was going to add "scary strong," but decided that was uncalled for. Beryllium was silent. Then she looked at Tinguely. Her eyes glittered unnervingly.

"You can call me whatever you want," Beryllium paused. "The global economy's on the ropes right now."

"Who threw cans on your yard?" asked Tinguely. Instead of Diet Coke, someone had thrown Budweiser beer cans into Beryllium's driveway. It looked very odd to have ten empty beer cans on a concrete slab.

"I don't know. Let's get back to the main question. The best way to make money these days is to do nothing. Book the money you would have lost if you had 'followed your gut' as a gain. It's all paper anyway. But, if you just have to gamble and lose, why not invest in gold?" she said. She paused. Tinguely's face was puzzled.

"All the talk show radio hosts recommend gold," said Tinguely.

Beryllium looked stern. "Tinguely, that was a joke."

"Did you know that most of the world's financial dynasties were born in bear markets?" pointed out Tinguely.

"Did you know that most aviation accidents are with small single-engine planes?" asked Beryllium.

"You fly a single-engine plane, right?" asked Tinguely. "Death wish or desire for speedy straight-line travel?"

"I hate talking in metaphors." Her mouth made a straight line. Beryllium's point of view was alien to Tinguely, who was a believer in "win-win." Further, for Tinguely, "straight-line travel" was anathema. She preferred to circle around until she had surveyed all the terrain at least a dozen times—close-up, far away, and sideways.

On the other side of Tinguely's house arose the sound of two pugs barking.

"Anyway, I got my start in crop-dusting," said Beryllium. Her smooth, dark hair flew away from the tight chignon.

"The chemicals are bad for animals, right? What would happen if, say, a couple of pugs were frisking about a field that was getting sprayed?"

Beryllium ignored Tinguely's question.

"So, you asked if I have a death wish? I always check the weather forecast before filing my flight plan. There's your answer."

"What is that supposed to mean?" asked Tinguely. She picked up a Diet Coke can and tried crushing it in her hands. She failed. "Who's throwing these things on my lawn? Yesterday there were two. Today there are four."

"Someone's been throwing the *Dallas Morning News* on my lawn. I don't want it."

"I'm thinking about buying 'distressed stock' that billionaires are having to unload when they get a margin call. I think there are some good deals out there. I read that one guy had to sell his stock that had once been worth $75.00 for $12.64. It's a good company. Everyone says it will go back up to at least $50 within a year."

"Vulture," muttered Beryllium under breath.

Beryllium's eyes looked hard and glassy as she said it. Not precisely like emerald. They seemed more alive than that. Tinguely thought of the eyes of a gecko or a Komodo dragon. She shuddered.

****

We all need an oracle. We need a soothsayer to project our own thoughts on so we can have some confidence in ourselves. Some people travel to Delphi. Some people frequent small storefronts with purple neon lights and a tarot deck poster in the window. Others call their old buddy who invariably buys high and sells low, ask him for advice, patiently endure his explanations of his "method," and then do the opposite. We all need an oracle.

****

It was another long, sleepless night. Tinguely was trying to read herself to sleep. It had been a fruitless day of trying to figure out which companies were tanking the fastest and hardest, and which billionaire owners might be vulnerable.

LouLou was preening herself and practicing her new phrase: "Wall Street Week: After the Break! Wall Street Week: After the Break!"

Tinguely glanced up from the book of Indian devotional songs to Shiva that she had been reading. Raised a Baptist and prohibited from dancing or having carnal thoughts, Tinguely found the idea of a deity who had erotic fantasies about Radha, a mortal cowherdess, disturbing, but weirdly irresistible.

She walked over to LouLou's cage and put a dark towel over it. She cooed to the parrot soothingly.

"LouLou. Lovely LouLou. Help me figure out how to get in on the margin call fire sales," she said.

LouLou squawked ungraciously. Tinguely changed her voice.

"Come, gentle night; come, loving, black-brow'd night … pay no worship to the garish sun," mumbled Tinguely. Lines from Shakespeare. *Romeo and Juliet.*

"After the Break! Wall Street Week!" squawked LouLou.

Tinguely sighed heavily and turned on the television. LouLou was a great companion, but noisy.

It was an infomercial. Tanned, with spiky brown hair, a button-down denim shirt, and khaki pants, a smugly overconfident spokesperson opened the door of his $80,000 sedan.

Infomercials were not her television viewing material of choice. But, since becoming addicted to forensic crime dramas, Tinguely had decided to allow herself to watch only C-SPAN and infomercials. C-SPAN was airing a rerun of last week's filibuster in anticipation of a vote to tax Medicare benefits.

Tinguely had already emailed her Congressmen to express her approval of the plan.

From her cage near the east window of Tinguely's bedroom, LouLou ruffled her feathers and noisily cracked open an almond with her beak. Next door, the neighbor's Westminster Kennel Club pugs, Jackson Heights and Jillian Lowes, were barking frantically.

Never mind it was 2:30 a.m.

"Call within the next fifteen minutes, and you can be a Registered, Certified DAY TRADER. In 24 hours, you'll be making trades, pouring the foundation of your new mansion. When the time comes and you want to buy your own island, we can help you with that, too."

Tinguely grabbed her purse with her credit cards, pulled out her cell phone and dialed the number. Jackson and Jillian appeared to be in mortal combat with an opossum, which was probably standing on the wooden fence, doing little more than baring its teeth and hissing.

Tinguely flashed on to an inspiration. Pharmaceuticals. The kind people get addicted to. Would that be a good stock to buy with leveraged funds?

Companies that made cheap caskets for all the increased deaths due to people unable to afford proper medical care, nutrition, prenatal care? This seemed like a winner.

In her corner still alert under the dark towel, LouLou cracked more nuts, ruffled her feathers again, and practiced a couple of her favorite sounds and phrases: first, the Friday

Noon Tornado Siren Test, and second, Tinguely's recorded voice on her answering machine greeting.

LouLou's squawky parrot voice emanated: "Sorry can't answer. Sorry can't answer."

****

It was morning and yet again, someone had thrown four empty Diet Coke cans on Tinguely's lawn. Beryllium was in her own yard, eyeing a soggy *Dallas Morning News*.

"Knowing there will be junk on the lawn is about the only thing that stays the same these days," commented Tinguely. "Hey, I made some money on Budget Casket stock."

"How? Surely there weren't a lot of margin calls with the owners of that stock," said Beryllium.

"Don't know. I sold short," said Tinguely.

"Whatever for? Oh, never mind. I got it," said Beryllium. "Shareholders see the future. Cremations are cheaper, hence no need for a casket—not even a cheap one from Budget Casket."

"Well, it went down all right."

Beryllium was changelessly gorgeous, with elegance and grace. Tinguely felt a bit intimidated. She looked down at the crushed cans in her hands.

"I guess I should make some sort of sculpture out of these," she said, thinking of Jean Tinguely, her namesake. If she truly followed his pattern, they would self-destruct in amusing ways. Tinguely didn't feel capable of doing anything amusing these days.

"That would be environmentally friendly. Not a bad idea," encouraged Beryllium. "I am very happy with the wind turbine projects. It seems to be a way to take the negative energy and chaos from the environment and turn it into something all of

us can use."

"Humanitarian?" asked Tinguely.

"Absolutely not. With all the changes and chaos in our wind, weather, and population patterns, wind turbines reintroduce order into Nature. They make the wind go in a certain way. They make things move together. We can see it. It's a mechanical choreography of the unruly forces of Nature. Heaven knows we need it."

"You're the one who has been throwing Diet Coke cans on my lawn!" It was an intrusive thought, articulated because of sleep deprivation.

Beryllium ignored her.

****

"Dad. I'm thinking about buying stocks. Paterfamilias Bank. Kerr-McGee Forest Products. American Motors. deChatville Mines. Mohawk Mills. Samson Equities. Ford Motor Company."

"Where are you getting these stock tips?" asked Dad. "Some of those companies haven't been around for fifty years."

"Where did they go?" asked Tinguely.

"Mergers. Acquisitions. Slow exsanguination in a bear trap."

"What?"

"It's what happens when the market goes down."

"That seems obvious, Dad. But these are household names."

"What have you been reading? *Look* magazine from 1953?"

"Uh. How did you know?"

"Are you getting enough sleep?"

"Will you take LouLou and the next door neighbor's

pugs?"

Tinguely hung up. In the space of a conversation, the pillars of something stable and strong had vaporized. The roof was falling in. The question was, the roof of what?

****

When everyone else is flying high, fly low.

When everyone else is flying low, fly high.

It's what bush pilots and WWI Sopwith Camel fighter pilots liked to say. The Sopwith Camel fighters liked to add, "Stay agile, even if your engines sputter and you think you're cutting out."

****

"I'm all for taxing Medicare payments," said Tinguely. She was explaining her rationale to her dad. Her dad had just turned 72.

"What's that?" Her dad sounded testy. He hated getting into these sorts of conversations with Tinguely on his cell phone during prime time. Nights and weekends were okay. Mid-week at three in the afternoon was not. "Tell me. In a nutshell."

"If you had to pay taxes on your MRIs, CT scans, PET scans, nanotube imaging diagnostics, exploratory surgeries, exotic animal-skin grafts, and fill-in-the-blank-oscopies, you'd probably think twice before having all that unnecessary stuff done, right?"

Her dad had just returned from his annual checkup with a fistful of orders for tests and lab work. Silence. Her dad did not respond.

"The worst part is, the imaging is so precise these days,

they'll always find something. Then they'll do expensive laser surgery, just to avoid a lawsuit later, just in case the anomaly—probably a stray lump of fat—that the radioactive nanotubes caused to light up, might turn out to be something serious," said her dad.

"Medicare should pay you NOT to take their tests. You're just another mark," said Tinguely. "Heaven help you if you're living in a government-subsidized nursing home and get a bad set of tests."

"That's right," agreed her dad. "Soylent green."

Soylent Green was her dad's favorite movie. Perhaps it was not his actual favorite movie, but it was the one he felt best depicted the way we would be living life in the very near future. In it, because of food and resource shortages, when people reached a certain age, they were euthanized. As they entered the chamber that took them to their final reward (being ground up and processed into a uni-food called "soylent green") uniformed waitstaff asked them politely, "What music would you like with your lethal injection?"

"Never let yourself or your kids get snookered into selling all your assets so you'll get 'free' state-paid nursing home care," continued Tinguely's dad.

"Yup. Soylent green."

The movie Tinguely felt most depicted the near future was *A Clockwork Orange*, but that was partially because she had studied Russian and liked the Russian-inflected Cockney slang, and partially because she half-expected the United States to announce a corporate merger with Russia, with the new capital being Anchorage, servicing 25% of the world's remaining oil reserves, which were conveniently located in the Arctic.

The infomercial caught her attention again. "Bear markets are mansion-makers. Dynasties."

****

Beryllium Markham was back. The Diet Coke cans had reappeared on the lawn. Beryllium seemed to have ignored the fact that Tinguely thought she was throwing them on her lawn.

Beryllium's lawn was pristine. There was a dew-sogged *Dallas Morning News* though. Tinguely wondered cynically if Beryllium had also thrown the newspaper on her own lawn and then soaked it with a water hose.

She must have seen Tinguely picking up Diet Coke cans. Beryllium's stained-glass door opened. She emerged, looking smooth and rested in slender black pants, a snowy-white long-sleeved blouse with bell sleeves, and slender patent black-leather boots. She wore a garnet necklace and matching earrings. Her fingernail polish had a salamander pattern.

Tinguely was wearing rumpled jeans, a faded Hawaiian t-shirt with silk-screened birds of paradise, and Cole Haan flats. Her hair was wet.

"Who's doing this?" asked Tinguely.

"How's your little stock market business coming along? Pick the flesh off any once-prosperous investors lately?"

"No," replied Tinguely glumly. "I always find out about them after they've already sold their stock due to margin calls and leveraged financing coming due."

"Well. Isn't that a shame." Beryllium held the soggy newspaper disdainfully between thumb and index finger.

"What's a derivative hedge?" asked Tinguely.

"Even if I knew, I wouldn't tell you."

Tinguely put the four empty Diet Coke cans into a plastic Lowe's Food Store bag and sighed. If truth were told, she was lonely.

Beryllium parted her lips in her glittering reptilian smile. Her lips were glossed the color of rubellite tourmaline.

****

Bears that dance are bears that bite. That was an old gypsy saying. They should know. They had perfected the art of the con where you use a dancing bear instead of a pickpocketing spider monkey wearing a little jacket and a tiny bellman's cap. "Dance with the bear!" Women in oversized t-shirts and stretch pants along with teenagers in "soldier boy" saggy pants would give it a try. The moment they jumped back from the suddenly snarling bear, their wallets and purses magically disappeared.

Bears that dance are bears that bite. If you doubt it, go to St. Petersburg. Take a stroll along Nevsky Prospekt along the banks of the Neva River.

****

The next few days were quieter than before.

Beryllium flew off to parts unknown.

Whoever was throwing Diet Coke cans onto Tinguely's yard decided to give her a break from picking up litter. The pugs barked only at night, and LouLou started sleeping during the day.

Tinguely got in the habit of drifting off to sleep sometime after lunch and awakening as the sun started to sink in the sky. During that time, she had vivid dreams. They were so odd that she remembered every one. She recorded each one in a journal.

The afternoon dreams seemed to have no pattern: thunderstorms with hail containing diamonds, dogs wearing silk booties, mechanical rats, a Humvee bearing a skull and crossbones pirate flag, quartz crystals from Hot Springs, Arkansas, a girl stepping out of a vintage Pepsi-Cola poster and coming alive, a small girl in a pink and green polka-dotted tricycle pedaling in tighter and tighter concentric circles. Finally, a Ring of Fire.

Thinking of the mechanical rats dream, Tinguely bought a contract to deliver a block of Victor Mousetrap stock.

She was not quite sure how buying and selling futures worked. Perhaps because she did not know, she made a tidy profit.

The Pepsi-Cola dream seemed too obvious. So Tinguely bought stock in Antiques Road Show. It zipped up during an afternoon surge, before plunging to a new low. Tinguely got lucky. She sold high.

As her sleep deprivation started to lift, Tinguely started to notice strange things about the transcribed dreams. The fragments of her dreams no longer seemed to correspond to company names, but they were coming together in two- and three-word clusters.

"Maybe it's an omen, LouLou," said Tinguely. She had let LouLou out of her cage, and the parrot was now contentedly nuzzling Tinguely's arm. "Maybe these are stocks I should be buying."

"Doggie Silk Booties. Diamond Hailstorm. Jolly Roger Humvee. Tricycle Toddler. The Sound of Sunlight."

Tinguely paused.

"Hmm. I don't quite get it. Well, with all the IPOs, who knows. Are they the titles of songs to be released? Or movies? Television series? BioPics?   Reality TV?"

Tinguely logged into her account on her computer and sold stock with Apple (iTunes) and Disney Studios. She did not actually own stock in either company.

"After the Break! After the Break!" squawked LouLou. She took a few steps across the table, cocked her head, and looked at Tinguely. Tinguely smiled.

"Crazy bird. You are too much. Want some dried

cranberries?"

In response to the cranberries, LouLou warbled and sounded oddly like a pigeon.

Tinguely wrote word combinations based on her dreams in her journal: *Crystal Rainbow Bracelet. Tiny Teddie. Poodle Bear Winkie. Oz Wonker. Celebrity Daisy. Fight My Fire.* The dream names were getting weirder and weirder.

Language was self-destructing. Was it amusing? Tinguely gazed on the pile of Diet Coke cans from her front yard. Unexpectedly, tears came to her eyes.

Not only were corporate identities melting, the language itself was encoding itself in a new way. Unleashed from their moorings on Wall Street and their once-solid footprint in the consciousness of the average American consumer, the things that had meaning no longer carried the same meaning. Reification processes once powered by image, advertising, code were now de-reification processes. This was no hard-charging bull market, where identity invented itself every day and then soared heavenward. This was a bear market. Entities and identities disintegrated.

For some people, the experience was weirdly liberating. And yet it could not help but reinforce existential isolation and a sense that discourse's links to meaning had broken down. Perhaps, this time, for good.

Tinguely was not sure at all what to do with the information. She checked the stocks she was to deliver. They had plunged with the Dow, which was down 250 points. She purchased Apple (iTunes) and Disney Studios.

She used the stocks she had just purchased to fulfill her commitment to deliver the stocks she had sold earlier in the day (at a higher price). It was a neat profit. Her hands were sweating.

"Dad. I have to learn how to sell short the right way," said Tinguely.

"Don't do it. You'll fry," said her dad.

"I don't care. I've got two weeks to make a mark. Bucks. It's going to happen."

"Keep your powder dry."

"Okay. So help me figure out what these omens mean. There's enough in it for all of us if we get it right," said Tinguely.

"Gambling is addictive, you know."

"This is not gambling. This is getting in touch with cosmic energies," said Tinguely.

"I think you need to talk to someone. You've been spending too much time alone."

"I've got LouLou."

"Exactly," said her dad.

****

Intrusive thoughts: Impulse? Give it up. Don't fight. Multifarious. Brutal.

> Winds and flowers bloom;
> The mind: ladybug or plain bug?
> Skeleton rosebuds.

> Old Dow Jones haiku

****

Russian President Dmitry Medvedev was making a speech.

A sidebar in the screen showed a clutch of Russian billionaires sitting glumly in a club in Stockholm.

A pale, bearded man was talking softly. "I hardly know who I am any more. I just don't see myself in the same way."

The television talk show host spoke. "These are the oligarchs, and the oligarchs took it on the chin. Margin calls. One guy had to liquidate all of his holdings in an auto parts distributor in Canada. He owned 20 percent. Imagine that. Overnight. Losing 20 percent of a company," the call-in television talk show host had a reverent voice, tinged with awe.

"How can a margin call do that?" asked a caller.

"Naked shorts." Long pause.

"Naked what? What's that?"

"He sold shares he didn't have. He thought he could cover it by buying cheap. But the price went up. Now he has to deliver. He has to buy the shares to deliver them. But he has no money. So, he has to sell every single stock he owns."

"Wow. Won't that flood the market? Drive the prices down?" asked the caller.

"Yes. But it won't do as much as naked swap-option derivatives," replied the host.

"What are those?"

"You don't want to know. You don't even want to know."

"Oh. Okay. By the way, doesn't Medved mean 'bear' in Russian?" asked the caller.

"Hehe. Yes. Oh. That reminds me—Ursula, the woman's name, must be derived from the Latin word for bear. *Ursa*."

"Hehe."

The Russian president finished his speech. Putin walked on stage. The people cheered.

****

Dreams changed. Not so clearly oracular.

Grass fires burned cars in the parking lot at Panera Bread

while Tinguely was waiting for her sandwich order.

The barista offered her two free cappuccinos for her patience while waiting for coffee while the restaurant was evacuated.

She was watching old 16mm films of old war movie with WWII veterans. Tinguely was organizing papers in her backpack as the old tape rolled. The projector was noisy. Her paper shuffling was noisier.

She couldn't find her car in the parking lot.

The more she was in a hurry, the more everything around her slowed: sandwich preparation, people evacuating the restaurant, the maze of fire trucks and blazing vehicles she had to cross to find her car, the pile of unsorted papers that grew and grew and grew

****

Dow Jones Haiku

(imagine the words / the syllable count, the "pop" / of insight and emptiness)

> Imagine the words
> The syllable count, the "pop"
> Insight, emptiness

****

CONVERSATION WITH DAD

FOX NEWS, FAIR AND BALANCED:
Albany, NY cityscape—a gorgeous sci-fi futurescape

of equidistant gray block skyscrapers, illuminated at night (fitting, of course, for the brainchild of a member of the Illuminati). Rodan, the beloved pterodactyl from 50s monster movies screeches and flaps her leathery wings. The "Egg" performing arts center starts to crack open, and a pterodactyl chick's beak pokes through.

Tinguely's "Notes to Self"

- What looks like greed on the surface is motivated by sadness, loss, loneliness.
- What looks like harshness (reptilian alien) is often one's projection of the self they wish they were … (hard, self-reliant, able to fly).
- Risk takes you into the world of the unreal.
- Omens and oracles: Are they projections? Are they not real? Or … are they are the real thing? And we are simply the shadow of them?

I'm not alone. Actually, I am. Not just existentially speaking. No. Correct that. 95 percent of the time I'm literally alone. Do I like it? I say "no," but I'm not really sure about that. There are so many things I take a stand on that isolate me.

Let's take Christmas songs as an example. I have taken a stand against any Christmas song post-1950. The fact I'm talking "Christmas" at all is, in itself, highly isolating via its offensiveness. I spent the holiday season in Azerbaijan where Christmas was a Santa Claus-inflected fashion statement for the London- and Houston-connected elite; had nothing at all to do with Orthodox views. I spent three holiday seasons in upstate New York, where "Christmas" triggered strife and discord as the cultural hegemony titans clashed and imposed a goofy gift-giving protocol that looked nothing like Eid or Christmas or Hanakkah or Kwanzaa. Ah yes. Holidays. No one should be alone during the holidays. I remember people saying that in Paraguay. Yet the existential isolation, coupled with the literal isolationist psychology made one profoundly alone, except with one's own ghosts and with one's own cultural forebears; usually shape-shifting liberators of the soul, who would allow you to at least envision the freedom to rampage, roam about, scamper, and indulge in flesh (werewolf or incubus – take your pick). And what pick I? Luison? Pombero? Kurupi? I'd choose the one who visits me as I sleep during siesta, lightly sweating, the fan evaporating the light film of sweat off my brow, soothing me, causing me to slip into the southern latitude-drugged slumber of a tropical rainforest afternoon.

I don't like the Christmas of today. I don't want to accommodate tunes that pander to the generations after the 1930s. Yes, I know I'm out of step. I'm retro in this regard. I want Christmas to be all about sepia tones and a fantasy of togetherness and/or angst that wax existential, not postmodern. On the tennis court, I try to have one thought per concept. The concept could be backhand. The concept could be forehand. Today, because I had not played in a week, my sole thought for forehand was "follow-through" – sometimes I fake follow-through. Fake Awake (no more). Must not stop the stroke when I think I'm directing it sufficiently. That will only cause "trampolining" – must smoothly and quickly follow ALL the way through – with authority. What's the single thought for backhand? Meet the ball WAY in front, and have the racquet down low and continental-gripped. When I do that, the ball has pace, power, and wacky spin. Serves? The one thought: continental grip; brush the ball; let it slice.

Tinguely Querer was lonely, despite the fact that when oil hit $140 a barrel, she had never been busier in her life. There was nothing like trying to drill oil wells in times of high demand and skyrocketing costs. Her BlackBerry buzzed constantly with text messages and emails. Still, she was lonely. The loneliness drove down to the rawest reaches of her soul.

The media was already calling it "Salmonella Summer." It was a sickness of unknown origin. Tinguely avoided tomatoes. Then she avoided jalapeños, chili peppers, tomatillos, pico de gallo, and then, finally, all kinds of fresh salsa.

Her nausea was not existential. It was not viral. Nor was it bacterial.

But did it matter at all?

Tinguely decided that it did not. She had to keep her mind on business at hand. She drove north on the highway, looked at the white, fluffy cumulus clouds, and wondered if the drought in the Panhandle would be over any time soon. Dorothea Lange's images of Okies in California—drought refugees—made the world think of drought in America in terms of ragged farmers running to their dugouts, a desiccated young migrant pea-picker holding out a Stoic face as she attempted to shield her children from the realities of malnutrition.

Drought in the new millennium meant adjustable rate second mortgages, high balances on credit cards, and streams of prerecorded, automated telemarketer phone calls starting around 4 p.m.

"Debt consolidators at your service! We will help you. Tired of phone calls? Our records show you own more than $6,000 on credit cards. Are you worried about how you'll pay? We will help you. We can stop the pain. Count on us!"

They had the wrong number. Tinguely did not carry balances on credit cards. The voice annoyed her. She tried talking to the recording in the hopes that it was voice-triggered to stop when some sort of sonic signature hit the equipment.

No such luck.

The recorded, disembodied telemarketer phone calls at dinnertime continued. The raw loneliness grew. The ache in her gut reached unspeakably ugly levels. She tried "re-scripting" the things she told herself. She tried chanting. She tried prayer.

All good. All ineffectual.

It was time to hit the road.

Tinguely was perversely grateful that she had to meet with the mineral owners that Bishoff, her dad's landman, had enraged by offering them a 3/16ths lease—just after the *Daily Oklahoman* ran an article advising mineral owners to never lease for less than 3/8ths. It was a typographical error, and the statewide newspaper printed a correction the very next day, but the damage was already done. Three-sixteenths was standard, but you couldn't tell the disgruntled owners, even though their mineral rights were miles from producing oil and gas fields, and even though it was unlikely that their acreage would ever be leased.

"Dad. I'll meet with the mineral owners. You can tell Bishoff we don't really need him on this. I can straighten it out," she said. She had already typed up a sheath of quitclaims and replacement leases.

The new documents were special for the landowners who insisted that the newspaper was right. She had something special for them. Quitclaims and replacement leases. 3/32nds lease.

32 is more than 8, right?

Tinguely smiled and pulled out five sets of steak knives and the three dozen "Believe In Yourself and All Things Are Possible" pocket diaries she had ordered, but then afraid to give out as Christmas presents after they struck her as vaguely blasphemous.

She wondered if she could get the mineral owners to write her a check to switch out the leases from 3/16ths to 3/32nds. Perhaps if she wore her business suit, jacket unbuttoned with a sheer chiffon blouse, push-up bra, and pearls underneath she could get some results.

No. That would be going too far.

Instead, she put her snub-nosed .38 in her purse, along with her concealed carry permit.

****

It was not a long drive, but it was a boring one. As Tinguely passed the Indian gaming joints, she tried to guess the vintage of each one.

Cherokee Nation Bingo was at least twenty years old. No one had bothered to update it. It had a special clientele that was not attracted to the casino a few miles to the north. That one had neon fireworks and a brand new sign: Cherokee Golden Thunder Gaming. It was about thirteen months old. The parking lot was always full.

One time she thought she saw her dad's white Suburban in the Cherokee Golden Thunder Gaming joint, but she knew she must be mistaken. At the time she spotted the vehicle, she was talking to her environmental activist friend, Chastain.

"Would your dad be drawn to risk and chance?" asked Chastain. Ever since she had spent nine months living on a platform near the top of an old-growth Ponderosa pine tree in Yosemite National Park, her diction was off.

"Oh, he likes gambling all right. He just prefers wildcatting. He can forestall for at least two years the fact that his method doesn't work. When you play the slots, you find out right away you've been deluding yourself," said Tinguely.

"I don't think that's how addiction works," said Chastain.

"The gambler thinks their method always works. They just haven't played long enough, or staked high enough."

"Oh." Tinguely did not quite follow what Chastain was saying, but she did not want to ask. She didn't want to hear Chastain's long, tangled disquisition.

The fact that the wheat farms her dad had purchased in northern Oklahoma near the Kansas border turned out to be a stunning investment annoyed Tinguely. The largest one was about twenty minutes from the Bison, Oklahoma-based Our Lady of Fatima shrine that Tinguely visited when she felt desolate and alone.

"I was right, after all. I am glad I did not listen to you," said Tinguely's father. She was mildly (and unpleasantly) surprised because he usually did not acknowledge that she had any independent thoughts or ideas. "I was right. I was more than right. I have built some equity—when wheat tripled, all the wheat farms doubled or tripled in value. Haha—Tintin, I'm telling you it feels good that you were wrong."

Tinguely shot a glowering smile once her dad's back was turned and he was exiting the room. She was glad he could not see her. He knew teeth-baring when he saw it.

Her dad was self-satisfied. He was gloating. He was smug—all because he was right—this one, single, solitary time.

She hated to be wrong.

****

For her 30th birthday, Tinguely purchased a vintage Chatty Cathy doll for herself, freshly minted circa 1963. The mouth was shaped into a smile as sweet as a peony, the tiny rubber teeth were perfectly formed and painted bright lead-oxide white.

For almost a full twenty minutes, Tinguely pulled Chatty

Cathy's talk string as she sat in the white-painted Early Americana Gazebo park bench in the manicured grounds of a small park in the shadow of a grain elevator in Bison, Oklahoma.

"You are my very best friend. I like you. Please take me with you. You are very nice. You are my best friend. Will you be my friend? Let's talk. You are my very best friend."

Chatty Cathy had a small bald spot in the back of her head where it appeared she had been dragged along the ground at some time in her life.

Otherwise, Chatty Cathy bore no signs of abuse. Her prim gingham dress was pristine, her baby doll collar a sweet, bleached white.

Tinguely pulled the string. Random, yet predictable. Who knew which phrase would come out? And yet, the phrase itself was utterly predictable.

Tinguely made a promise to herself that, when faced with pressure or uncertainty, she would limit her own conversation to an inventory of 10 or 15 favorite phrases.

"You are very astute. I understand. I am listening. Would you like coffee or a bottle of water? These are uncertain times. You can do it. I believe in you. You are very astute."

****

She had opposed the purchase from the very beginning. "It's too risky. It's in the middle of nowhere. I know this country. I once got stuck up to the axle in mud and had to be pulled out by a farmer and his huge tractor. Thank goodness he was around. You can't even get a cell signal up here."

"We'll need the land for the equipment yards once we start developing the field I've got mapped out. If my calculations are correct, we'll be drilling at least twenty wells. Oil and gas, but primarily gas."

When her dad bought the farms, land was cheap. The closest oil well—a part of the Cherokita Trend—was at least five miles away. Wheat prices were low. Jobs and industry were steering clear of the short grass prairie, the "Red Carpet Country" wheat growing region, which lay hours from the closest "big box store" strip mall or high-speed Internet connection.

Rising demand, limited supply, hedge fund purchasing, short selling, and other forms of speculating drove the price of oil sky-high.

"I feel I'm in some sort of 'Farmer in the Dell' hell," said Tinguely to her dad, who was not listening. "The price of oil goes up, and then stimulates the production of ethanol, made from corn. Corn goes up. Ethanol millionaires buy up farmland. They move south. They buy up wheat farms. They drive up the price of wheat farms."

Tinguely's dad started to pay attention as the conversation moved to wheat and oil. They were getting ready to go into the Bar-S Grill for a late lunch before going back out to the field. This was wheat country, too, and the parking lots were full of brand new pickups and SUVs. A man got out of black pickup with a white sign on the door: "Jake's Tools."

"I wish I had bought a few more of the farms while I had a chance—especially if they were selling the minerals along with the surface," he said. "The Mortson place, and also the Kladzuba farm. Oil, primarily."

"The only people who can afford them now are the big boys—Shell, BP, Exxon-Mobil—or the wind farm guys," said Tinguely.

"We need to start drilling before drill pipe gets even more expensive. The Chinese are raising the price of steel. It's up 60 percent," said Tinguely's dad.

"The rat eats the cheese." The Farmer in the Dell song was going through Tinguely's head. She could not quite remember the lyrics though.

"What?" said Tinguely's dad.

"The cheese stands alone. The cheese stands alone," hummed Tinguely under her breath.

"I still did not hear you," he said.

"You are very astute," said Tinguely. In her head, Chatty Cathy was saying, over and over, "You are my very best friend."

Tinguely's dad watched her take the Chatty Cathy out of the backpack where she was keeping it.

"Where'd you pick up that old thing? Someone's trash?"

****

She met him at the Flying J truckstop just off I-40, where crews were still cleaning up high-wind damage. Someone said it was a tornado, but the meteorologists at the National Severe Storms lab said no. Doppler radar indicated straight winds. There had been no characteristic "hook echo." But what about the eye-witnesses who saw the funnel drop from the clouds? It did not count. You can't trust your eyes. You have to go with what you can measure. The Doppler radar is based on echoes. On sound. That is all that really counts.

He was standing in line waiting to pay for a bottle of Coke and to purchase a pack of Marlboros.

"Pull-string talking doll," she muttered under her breath. "You're perfect. You're absolutely perfect."

He was slender, tall, athletic, with warm, ginger tones in his skin. She felt rivalry and competition until she heard him speak.

"I love the way you think. I love your anger. You make me smile. I understand. I feel the same way."

His hair was platinum. His lips were full. His eyes were

dark, compassionate, warm. In contrast with her father, he actually listened to her. He followed her line of thinking, her arguments. She understood that he dealt with existential angst by emitting a torrent of words.

Thankfully, they were ones she could listen to over and over and over again.

"I love the way you think. I love your anger. You make me smile. I understand. I feel the same way."

Somewhere the meteorologists detected a hook echo somewhere over the prairie where no one saw even the slightest hint of rotation.

****

High commodities prices resulted in high food prices. Smaller portion sizes became the norm in restaurants. You'd think people would lose weight, thought Tinguely.

She looked bitterly at her thighs. She had started to consider them massive. They were not, but they had increased in girth.

"You look nice," the man with the platinum hair said. "You have a real woman's body."

Tinguely took in his words without registering emotion.

Under her breath, "It is a blessing and a curse."

He was drinking a green tea frappucino from one of the surviving Starbucks in that part of Oklahoma. She was drinking tap water from an old Panera Bread coffee cup. Tears welled up in spite of her determination to maintain equanimity. A woman with Lycra-enhanced denim walked by her, her thighs chattering as the fabric slapped against itself.

She wondered where his pull string might be; how she could make him say the nice things she so enjoyed hearing in their last encounter.

He pulled out a pack of cigarettes and searched for a lighter.

He came up empty.

"I have a souvenir pack of matches," said Tinguely. "From the Baku Radisson. Everyone smokes there."

He looked her questioningly.

"I don't smoke. Never did. But I love the place." She paused as she thought about Azerbaijan and the deep turquoise waters of one of the deepest inland seas. "I liked the view—the Caspian Sea from the City Lights lounge on the 18th floor. I could look down on Ichiri Sheher—the old city—and see the Maiden Tower," she said. She fumbled for the matches, and then handed them to him.

He still said nothing. She handed him the matches. They walked outside. He lit his cigarette. She blurted out words as though a pull string in the back of her neck had been pulled a dozen or so times.

"You are right. You are always right. Your mental energy is amazing. You have nice eyes. Nice abs. You are always so brilliant. I love your thoughts. Nice pectoral muscles. Nice quadriceps. Good. Great. You are brilliant. Thank you. You are nice."

****

Tinguely bid on a pull-string talking toy on eBay and won it. It was a See 'n Say toy, which had pictures of farm animals. The day it arrived in the mail was the day she realized she needed to get new tires for her 5-speed Volkswagen Passat.

"Pig. Oink oink oink oink." The voice was soothing, the animal sound was amusing. Tinguely smiled.

She bought a membership at Sam's Wholesale Club so she could get her four tires at a discount. The guy who took her order was talking about going to Australia.

"I'm going to give myself a month to find a job. I want

to try it out there. There is more to this world than this." He waved his hand dismissively.

Tinguely wondered if he had ever tried Buddhist meditation. *Om.* It had a resonance that was supposed to trigger cause and effect in the universe. At least that was how Tinguely came to understand it.

She looked down at the See 'n Say pull-string talking toy. She pulled the string.

It did not contain chanting or Buddhist meditative phrases. Tinguely did not notice.

"Cow. Mooooo."

"Dog. Arff arff ruff ruff grrrr."

Does it ever seem odd to you that many of the world's civilizations were pyramid builders?

How did they all happen upon that particular architecture? Every child who has ever experimented with blocks has found that the most stable edifice is a pyramid, so perhaps it's not so earth-shattering as it may seem that so many people decided to try their hand at a pyramid.

But still, why is it that they seem to have so much in common?

What if the solutions are in the stars?

Let's think about this.

Back in 1,000 BC, the stars were absolutely brilliant. They were bright. The constellations were absolutely in your face. Imagine the brilliant night of a full moon. The moon could be so bright there could be moon shadows. It's hard to imagine from the vantage point of today's cities.

Brilliant stars, maps in the skies. The night sky was so fascinating I'm sure that during the new moon people dragged around exhausted during the day after staying up all night watching the skies.

What were they watching?

What if they were looking at star-based blueprints? What if there were blueprints for buildings, structures, etc? Okay – and let's get more extreme – what if the sky was yesterday's Internet, a shared repository of image-based knowledge? Images blended with oral traditions. It was a scary time. Very little was written, scratched in stone, or carved into cuneiform.

Forget MP3 files. Forget AVI. Forget everything that could be made dead, like paper.

With digital spontaneity, are we more like the stargazers than the Francis Baconian "New Scientists" Royal Society types? A printed page is static.

Oral tradition and knowledge gleaned from the ever-moving skies are fluid and aggressively mediated by society and human desire.

Knowledge gained through social networking is fluid, ever-evolving, mediated by human desire (and tools – technology).

Tools of transmission: technology.

Ancient technologies? Tools of transmission – what were they? The stars themselves, but oral tradition – frozen (and ultimately misrepresented) by glyphs, cuneiform, diagrams, art.

"Tinguely, we need to get into ICE-9." Tinguely's dad was talking to Erneiro, a Brazilian geologist who was in the Texas panhandle to take a course on salt tectonics. Erneiro specialized in structures that tended to be at depth and, when it came to offshore Brazil, in fantastically deep waters.

"Who gave you that idea?" asked Tinguely suspiciously. She glowered at Erneiro, but immediately brightened when her scowl caught his eye. She had just finished creating an illustrated version of Kurt Vonnegut's *Cat's Cradle*, and the final image—of all the world's oceans frozen by the new form of water, dubbed ICE-9—was chilling to create.

Erneiro beamed her way. His smile was wide. Tinguely shuddered. He would offer to teach her Kizomba again. She had already learned it in Angola, but no matter. He would not listen.

The idea of Brazilian platforms frozen fast in an eternal tableau of ice was somehow cheering.

"ICE-9 is the conference that will be held next year in Rio de Janeiro. We've been invited to set up an exhibit," said Dad.

"Oh. Of what?"

It was Dad's turn to glower.

"Of our new fields, which we discovered with our new technologies, of course."

"Of course." Tinguely tried to make her voice sound bland. Dad was sensitive to sarcasm.

****

Although she cringed at the idea, Tinguely had become addicted to listening to conspiracy radio. It was so compelling she found herself driving out of her way just so she could continue listening. She also found she looked forward to six-hour drives to the Texas Panhandle, precisely because she knew it meant almost a half a day of soothing short-grass prairie-scape and boundless skies.

The predicating assumption of talk radio was that you could never let down your guard, never relax. Instead, you had to brace yourself for traffic stops and the inevitability of incarceration. Nice thought? No. But you had to live with it. After all, the world's secret societies were/are plotting to enslave you. Is this unrealistic? Paranoid? Any student of history would say no. After all, the Catholic Church had just the same ultimate aim. Just ask Voltaire. Just ask Rabelais—and he should know—he was part of the crowd.

The talk show hosts had talent. They were amazing. They could take the most innocuous and boring training exercise and turn it into evidence that another level had been achieved—another stage reached in the grand plan of the world's wealthy to enslave and humiliate the American middle class as they stripped them of their assets and freedom.

On the other hand, they spoiled their message a bit by hawking gold coins and desiccated, freeze-dried foodstuffs with ten-year-storage guarantee.

Tinguely's aunt bought into the paranoia in the late 1970s and bought a five-year supply of raisins, powdered milk, date sugar, dry soup mix, and texturized vegetable protein (soybean cooked, formed, and freeze-dried to approximate/mimic ground meat).

After six or seven years, it was, in a word, inedible, despite the fact it was supposed to have a shelf life of something like a quarter century.

It's not easy to change gears. Sit down all day, in meetings, looking focused on the computer – then, at 9 p.m., suddenly change gears to play tennis. Does that work? I am not going to be angry with myself for playing badly, for never quite warming up, and making my tennis buddies marvel at how far I've declined in my abilities to hit the ball, cover the court. To be honest, I think I was playing adequately, everything considered. I'm going to focus on just three things when I'm on the court: Forehand? Hit with authority and follow through all the way. Backhand? Hit with authority and make sure I'm hitting it far in front of me. Serve? Slice serve. Hit it high, keep my head up, and follow through. Think about timing. Lee Ann thought my serve looked better toward the end. It was not really better – I was just going back to my old habitual "it is what it is" kind of serve that at least got it in the service box. But it had no spin, and it was easy for her to just plunk it back over the net where I could not possibly get it back.

Anyway. It was exercise. That is good. I'm in touch with my mortality these days. I'm in touch with everyone's mortality, it seems. My mother passed away – it's only been two and a half months, but it feels like a long, long time ago. I feel myself having a rush of sadness at the very thought of it. On the 13th it will have been three months. Just sad. Too sad. The last time I talked to my sister, she talked about how she could not go on. It was too much for her. She said she was just too overwhelmed and that she was having suicidal thoughts. Mortality – well, we're just so lucky when we are of sound body and mind. We might as well live it up – feel good about ourselves. And do what we can to live our lives in ways that make us aware that we're living – not just driving along insensate ... what would I do if I had no fear? What would I do if I truly believed that God would take care of me? I can tell you that, absolutely and definitively, I would have my own company; I'd build a little

consulting business and then start working on humanities/
heart journal opencourseware, and I'd also start writing
more ... and I'd attempt to keep my existential anxiety to a
minimum by keeping a baseline of work, but not exceeding
that. I would play tennis twice a day – once working on
serves and working with the ball machine; the others with
drills and/or scrambles ... playing with various ladies....

I don't have any great illusions about my tennis abilities
... I think I have a pretty firm glass ceiling. Plus, I don't
want to reduce myself to being all about sandlot tennis
and doing anything to win – despite form ... I know talking
about tennis does not seem to relate to the bigger issues of
life, but I have to say I think it does.

The other day I watched a documentary about The Flaming
Lips – an Oklahoma City band – one I like to think of as a
"spectacle band" in the sense that they seem to be all about
crazy, over-the-top theatrics – a spectacle of exaggeration
and juxtaposition – that is about distorting/perturbing
consciousness itself, aggressively without drugs; the
members of the band, who were deeply addicted, were
not really contributing to the surrealist CECI NE C'EST PAS
UN PIPE kind of mind-bending surrealism ... not Dalì, but
Magritte, n'est pas? Well, who knows. Play tennis, and
think of the court as facets of a blood diamond. The fact
you have leisure time makes you culpable of something – of
a kind of insensitive solipsism ... should you not be aching
and swallowing mud, illiterate and superstition-charged
– rather than be whining about your lack of leisure time? I
don't know.

Mortality makes one reassess. Then it makes you retreat
from your reassessment in order to not have to confront
those uncomfortable truths.

It is time to go.

It's just hard.

Full moon. Dark sky with light wispy clouds over the moon's face of craters. Tinguely Querer was driving in the middle of the high plains. She heard yaps of coyotes and yowls of something feline. A dark, feral shadow lurked along the edge of the blacktop county road, with gravel shoulder. Was it a chupacabra? Tinguely shivered. Would the chupacabra smell her clammy, perfumed sweat, chase her down, feed on her blood, and to swallow her soul?

The cattle guard rattled as she drove over it to enter a dark, shambling ranch. She hoped it was the Freestoner Ranch. She had been looking for it and wanted to approach Mr. Freestoner to sign him up for an oil and gas lease.

****

"Monkey's Paw or Death Ruby?" asked the man wearing a faded red bandanna, narrow boot-cut Wrangler jeans, a jean jacket, and rodeo belt buckle. He looked like the kind of cowboy you'd never see in a cowboy movie. He was too weather-beaten. His eyes were vaguely feral. His nose was all the way wild, totally coyote.

"If given the choice, and you HAD to make a choice, which would you go with?" he asked. "Monkey's Paw or Death Ruby?"

"What are they anyway?" asked Tinguely. She had driven seven hours, non-stop from central Oklahoma, and was in no mood for cryptic, Yoda-like pronouncements from a retro cowboy washed up on the beach sands of time.

"And imagine you can't say no. You can't refuse to choose."

"Mr. Freestoner, I have the documents ready for you to

execute. You'll be glad you did this." She wanted to get it over with. Drive to Amarillo. Get a room at a comfortable discount version of upscale hotels. The idea of lying on a soft mattress at a Hyatt Place or a Marriott Courtyard seemed more important than anything else at this point.

"Ma'am, Mr. Freestoner's been dead for 10 years."

"What?" Tinguely was not amused. "How did I miss that? I checked the records myself. I never make mistakes like this."

"I'd say this was a pretty big one," said the cowboy, unsympathetically. "So. Ma'am. What would you do? Which would you choose?"

"Sir. I think I'd choose the one that would get me away from this place as quickly as possible." He looked crestfallen. "Sorry. I don't mean to be rude. I'm just really tired. And this means I'm going to have to go back, recheck records, reissue leases and drafts."

"The Monkey's Paw grants you three wishes, but each one comes with horrific price. You'll pay. Yes, missy, you'll pay. But the Death Ruby's no bargain. The Death Ruby will make you fabulously wealthy. But all who touch it, except for the owner, die."

"That's easy," said Tinguely, still annoyed. "I'd go with the Death Ruby. Good secret weapon. I'd be rich. Good way to get rid of the competition."

"For having such a sweet face, you sure have some mean thoughts," said the cowboy.

"You haven't heard the half of them," said Tinguely. "Got any coffee around here? It was a long drive, and, to tell the truth, I'm in a bad mood."

"You don't say," said the cowboy. "See you at the bunkhouse."

"By the way, I'm not sure I quite buy it that the owner of a Death Ruby stays healthy. I would think that everyone would eventually be killed by the thing. Some people more quickly than others."

"Think what you want," said the cowboy. "I wouldn't want to tangle with you, though."

****

"Sign up Freestoner. Then, keep going. See if you can get information. We've got a chance to lease Morrell's granddaughter's interest. I'd like to find the location, drill a new well, and test the formations. It will be good for all of us if it works out," said Dad.

"What makes you so sure?" asked Tinguely. Why not leave well enough alone? Something was wrong with the story she had been told. Something was behind the scenes, between the lines.

Tinguely pulled up to the rock-and-mortar ranch house. The clock on her dashboard said 4:40 p.m. She took her keys out of the ignition of the Blazer she was driving. The keys felt cold and metallic in her hand.

She walked under a stunted sycamore tree. The ranch house and office were on the edge of a wash or, as the locals called it, an arroyo. That meant there were a few trees.

Acquiescing to the cowboy's insistence that she take a look around the ranch, Tinguely attempted to mind her manners. It was not easy.

Cattle shuffled slowly, mesmerized by the wind turbines spinning round and round, silently, slowly, both positive and negative, in direct response to the currents of cold air flowing down from the north in North America's most prominent wind corridor.

"If you'll pour me a cup of coffee, I'll work on it while you show me around," said Tinguely. She fully expected coffee the consistency of tar and the pH of battery acid. She was pleasantly surprised that it was fresh, tasted like caffe americano—espresso shots with hot water.

She was in the middle of a ghost ranch. No one had the courage to admit what it was, but Tinguely Querer knew immediately.

At first, she wondered if the cowboy she was talking to was a phantom. She realized, after he drank boiled "cowboy coffee" with the grounds at the bottom of the mug, unrolled a yellowed newspaper from 1955, then started talking about how people had started buying up all the water rights to the Ogallala Aquifer, that there was really no way of knowing. His language hinted at transporting people from Mexico. He could be an apparition from the past. He could be from right here, right now. He could be a strange living outlier rafted in on a glacier of time. He could be the bones of a memory to be held by someone sometime in the future. Who could know?

"Have to admit, it's nice to have company for a change," said the cowboy. "Oh, and by the way, my name's Chance."

"I'll bet people called you 'Lucky' when you were a kid," said Tinguely. She realized she needed to sound folksy. Sometimes being down to earth came easily to her. Sometimes, though, it didn't. At times, she seemed standoffish or detached—something like a process server, paid for putting her emotions in a bucket by the door.

"Nope. I never was," he said. "That was the cat. Now he was lucky."

Tinguely smiled. If she could, she'd put her emotions, not in a box or a bucket, but in an air-sick bag. There was something warm about the breeze, although the air was chilly.

****

"Dad, if you're going to buy anyone's mineral rights, or buy the surface so you can lease it out to wind turbine companies, you're going to have to chum the waters."

"Throw bloody, cut-up fish into the waters? Draw the sharks?" asked Dad, incredulously. "Why would we want to attract the sharks?"

"Because after they've fed, they'll lead us to the live fish," said Tinguely.

"Why would we want live fish?"

"Dad," said Tinguely, suddenly exasperated. "I'm speaking metaphorically."

"I wouldn't if I were you."

"What? Speak metaphorically?"

"Right. Don't underestimate the ranchers and their families. You're not giving them any credit for intelligence. More than one city slicker has found this out, much to their dismay. You're about as city slicker as they come, Tinguely."

"Dad, I don't know who or what it is that you see when you look at me and talk to me, but I'm telling you, it's not at all the way I perceive myself. Give me some credit, Dad."

"Do the people who chum the waters ever get bitten by the sharks they're trying to trick?"

"No. Never," said Tinguely, straight-faced. "When you baited a trap, did you ever catch anything you didn't want?"

"Absolutely." Dad paused. "I learned a lot from that."

"Gotta go. The cowboy said he has some apple cobbler for dessert."

"Thought you were going to spend the night in Amarillo."

"The air is fresh and clear. Amazing."

She clicked "end call" on her BlackBerry.

****

Cattle silhouetted against the setting sun. The clouds were

spectacular. An antique windmill used to bring water from the aquifer to the surface rattled and creaked in the wind.

Cattle moved together. They seemed to move toward the water. Then they moved en masse in another direction. They seemed to be moving away from the rays of orange-pink light shooting across the horizon.

Tinguely, watching them, fell into a reverie. Then blinked. The cattle. Were they moving? Were they retreating? Tinguely could swear they were shuffling slowly, softly—backwards.

Blink.

A look down at the coffee cup. A quick rundown of what she had eaten. Mushrooms? No. Brownies? No. "Herbal" tea? No.

****

There was something about the earth-colored farmhouse and the bright white wind turbines set along the fence line in the direction of prevailing breezes that gave Tinguely pause. A face flickered at one of the windows. Wisps of clouds cast specters (or shadows) on the smooth prairie cover. Cattle grunted to each other. When the grass waved in the breeze, the clouds seemed to edge backwards, against the direction of the wind.

Tinguely braced herself. There was something here. It was making her uneasy.

The property was located in the shadow of the old XIT Ranch in the Texas Panhandle north and west of Amarillo. From 1885 to 1912, the ranch encompassed more than three million acres. There were around 300 windmills. 150,000 head of cattle grazed on the XIT Ranch lands. They were tended to by hundred of cowboys.

Ordinarily, Tinguely would not be anywhere near this part of the Panhandle, but supposedly a deep well had been drilled here during one of the booms, and the drill cuttings streamed oil, with strong odor of gas. The operator, Karlton Morrell, who had also owned a large part of the former XIT Ranch, had run out of money. The well cost a lot more than he had bargained for. But it would pay off. He just needed to raise money. So, while he set out to raise money to continue drilling and complete the well, Morrell had done his best to suppress the information. He had hoped to sell his remaining interest in the ranch and then do the completion.

The poor guy never had the chance. His shiny black Ford pickup was found in a ravine. He was nowhere to be seen. In fact, he was never anywhere to be seen from that day on. He disappeared.

"Dead, most likely," said Dad. "Quite a shame. Morrell was a good guy. I always liked him."

The sky was the blue of childhood storybooks. The prairie switchgrass was the straw-gold of memory. The roof was the slate gray of long-forgotten dreams.

****

"Say, Chance, what is it like living in a ranch house that was abandoned a hundred years ago?" asked Tinguely. It was dark. It would be a dangerous drive back to Amarillo, due to mule deer and coyotes. Road hazards.

"Nothing I'd recommend for someone like you," he said.

"I can handle myself. I've done a lot of fieldwork. Had to. Geology degree," said Tinguely. There was something about this wizened old cowboy that got under her skin.

"That's why I would not recommend it. If you've ever done anything you wish you hadn't in your life, you're not going to have an easy time of it around here, once the moon's up and the wind carries the voices."

"What voices?"

"Coyote."

"That's nothing."

"And the whispers. The whispers that come up from inside of you and swirl around your inner ear."

"Okay, that's enough for me for tonight." Tinguely stood up. "Thanks, Chance. I'm heading back to Amarillo."

"Yup. You are," he said.

"What is that supposed to mean?"

"It's where you started out, after all. You don't have much choice in the matter, as far as I can tell."

"Well, maybe. You're right. It's where I had my first job." She noticed he had a smooth wooden box in his hand. He stood up and made a motion to give her the box.

"Well, Miss Tinguely, please take this with you. It's a present from the ranch."

"Wow. It's beautiful. An antique cigar box?" The gift was so unexpected that Tinguely was taken by surprise. She was touched. The soft sentiment was quickly replaced by suspicion. "What's inside? A Monkey's Paw? A Death Ruby?"

"Heck hek hek." Chance's cackle was not exactly a laugh. "Just a souvenir cigar box from old XIT Ranch. Thought you might like it."

Tinguely accepted it and opened the lid gingerly, half-expected a bat to fly out. The box was empty. Inside, the wood was burned with the XIT brand.

"Thanks, Chance. You're a nice guy. This was very generous of you."

"Heck hek hek," he laughed again. "Here's a thermos of that coffee you liked so much. Watch out for the mule deer."

She got back to the vehicle. The time: 11:45 a.m. Tinguely checked her watch. Time: 10:45 p.m. In the space of her vehicle, time had run backward. She looked at the second counter. Time was, indeed, going in reverse.

Foreclosure

The three dozen or so abandoned, foreclosed houses had turned into moldering ghost houses, their yards a fetid jungle. Swamp gas clung to storage sheds and half-drained swimming pools.

Tinguely Querer caught a glimpse of something much too shiny and smooth to be a dog, but too large to be a goat, cow, or pony. It slipped through the dark, waxy leaves of an unpruned magnolia tree, with what appeared to be a large, possibly prehensile tail, curling waggishly through the lower limbs.

The sound of raspy breathing and tree limbs cracking came from the magnolia. Although Tinguely was intensely curious, she decided not to pursue the animal. It did not seem to be a very good idea. The sounds continued and seemed to ascend the tree. Then, with a crash of branches and leaves, the sound stopped.

Dusk was falling. The Pinella Pines Subdivision she had been hired to survey was full of abandoned homes, repossessed in the mortgage crisis. The homes were all less than ten years old, but the subdivision had a jungly, noir feeling. For every home with lights burning in the dining rooms, and citronella candles burning on the decks or around the pool, five or six had been either vandalized by owners angry over their suddenly unaffordable ballooning ARMS, and another half dozen were simply left behind.

****

Her cell phone startled her.

"Hey kitty-cat, how are you doing?" It was the voice of a guy Tinguely had met in the office of her latest client.

He had taken to calling Tinguely "Hello Kitty" or simply "Kitty" after he saw the Hello Kitty post-it notes she used to remind herself of dates to enter into her calendar. She had bought them because they were the only post-it notes she could find in the strip mall where she grabbed coffee one afternoon.

Tinguely thought of Hello Kitty backpacks, toasters, and pencil cases she saw in Hello Kitty stores in Osaka. She remembered the photo of a child soldier in Liberia who used a Hello Kitty backpack as a lucky charm. He also wore a cheap blonde chemotherapy wig. It was supposed to bring health.

"Hey, Kitty, Hello Kitty," said the voice on the phone.

Tinguely smiled.

****

Then her dad called.

She listened for awhile, not responding. Then her words came out, blurting.

"Dad. I think I had a vision last night. Sabotage. Key bridges and dams. I've started to wonder about the bridges and dams here. Commerce, security, fear, death," Tinguely told her dad. "I don't believe, but then I do care."

The connection was bad. She could not hear his reply.

She glanced at the television. Then a *USA Today* headline caught her eye. A Senate subcommittee had just heard testimony on the impact of infrastructure sabotage across America.

Tinguely's stomach clenched. Something scritch-scratched against the wall. It was a large gecko. Its tongue flickered, then it ran out the open doorway and into the hall.

****

After one week without air conditioning in the thick central Florida mangrove heat, a peculiar slimy mold started to coat the carpets, and mildew blackened the grout in the bathrooms. The 2800 block of Periwinkle Way, a cul-de-sac that bordered a small park and a "green belt" area, seemed to be the worst. The former owners had not vandalized their homes, or stripped them of anything they could pawn or install in a parent's home. Instead, they seemed to have left them in haste. In some cases, in mid-meal.

The large bank stuck with the properties was investigating reports of possible environmental damage around the repossessed homes.

The shadowy creature appeared again. Whatever it was definitely had four legs, a tail, and a head. But, what was it? It was much too low to the ground to be a dog. It was not shaped like an alligator. Just as Tinguely caught another glimpse, it dashed back into the shadows between two pale brick ranch-style homes. Something seemed to be scaling the wall, running up the kudzu that had started to overtake the south edge of the three-bedroom, two-bathroom mother-in-law plan ranch.

*****

Headline: Seven-foot Nile Monitor Lizard In Our Town?

Photo Caption: The Nile Monitor is a vicious predator that will eat anything that fits in its mouth.

Question: What were Nile Monitor Lizards doing in Florida? What started out as a cute birthday present turned into a large, smelly reptile that could escape virtually any cage, climb up walls, and scamper out open windows, doors, and cat doors.

The wildlife disappeared. The owners forgot about them.

No one thought anything of it.

That is, until they started feeding on neighborhood livestock (dogs, cats, rabbits, songbirds, toddlers).

*****

Tinguely pulled up to the hotel in a rented Ford Mustang. The car was new, with only 8,000 miles on it, but was already missing various knobs and part of the dash was brittle as though they had used the low-density polyethylene instead high-density— or was it the other way around?

Toothless tiger.

Tinguely remembered when the Mustang was a hip, strong muscle car. You have to go back to 1966 for that, she thought. What happened in those forty-something years? That was two generations back.

Uncle Chunk used to brag that he had a Mustang. That was when Tinguely's father was making his first millions in oil, gas, wheat, and gold. That was when a million dollars was a staggering amount. Now, one would have to earn ten times that, and she would still not be rewarded with the shock and awe that seemed fitting.

Uncle Chunk's Mustang came from Tinguely's dad's largesse. He bought it for him as a graduation gift. It was a classic car, already more than twenty years old in 1987, when Uncle Chunk demonstrated that he, too, could somehow swim the weird and turbulent waters of male self-fashioning.

Nostalgia is cruel.

Tinguely's graduation gift from dad was a copy of Stephen Covey's *The Seven Habits of Highly Successful People*, and a collectible "rare book"-rated copy of Spenser's *The Faerie Queene*. Her mom gave her a check for $50. She used it to buy new windshield wiper blades for her rusty old Volkswagen

Rabbit, and to go on a three-day carbohydrate binge, eating and drinking nothing but *postres mexicanos* and syrupy hazelnut frappucinos.

"Struggling builds character," said Dad.

Tinguely balefully considered her Uncle Chunk.

Perhaps he could set up an offshore banking enterprise on Barbados. Tinguely noted with satisfaction that Chunk's skin was already getting very leathery from too much subtropical sun. Chunk should avoid the sun. His ancestors (and Tinguely's, for that matter), hailed from the Pyrenees between France and Spain. They came to trade in mink, beaver, and sometimes wolverine.

Sometimes Tinguely craved hot chocolate and goose liver pâté. She assumed it was utterly atavistic. One of these days, her atavism could cause her to think of impaling a captor's head on a stake and anchoring it on an upended pike.

For now, the hide of the moose someone in her family had shot, skinned, and tanned would have to do.

"You have to send a message," she said. "Otherwise, you're no longer the hunter. You're the hunted."

****

Someone started shipping exotic animals to pet stores in America, even though, in theory, no one in their right mind would want a black mamba, king cobra, Nile Monitor lizard, Komodo dragon, Burmese python, or anaconda in their teenage son's bedroom.

Someone started shipping people to the Americas, even though, in theory, no current inhabitant in his or her right mind would want a fur trapper, clear cutter, distributor of smallpox-infected blankets, or wooden stockade builder to settle there, in the current inhabitants' pristine and nicely-balanced ecosystem.

****

The Mustang hurrumphed to a stop. Injectors need cleaning? Too much ethanol in the gas blend?

Dusk had turned to night. Tinguely opened the car door and uncoiled her legs. They were tense and a little sore from too many squats at "Pump and Crunch" class.

The air was thick with humidity. For seemingly no reason at all, she felt a surge of aggression. Startled, she sat back in the car, closed the door and breathed deeply. When she felt aggression, it was usually a response to fear. What was out there? All she could hear were her own deliberate exhalations.

****

Seated in a corner of the outdoor café, Tinguely contemplated the wrought iron gates. The pillars were covered with coiled ivy and vines. It was dark. Tinguely was drinking coffee and slowly eating a cheese quesadilla when she heard the creep and crunch of something moving in the parking lot.

A thin man—a Praying Mantis in a limp t-shirt and gym shorts, spiky gray hair—appeared, then disappeared into the shadows.

Tinguely moved into the shadows so that she would not be detected. Her muscles flexed instinctually. He appeared thin, weak, alone. So alone and vulnerable, he would be an easy catch. For some reason, his presence made Tinguely think of death squads operating in Nicaragua during the 1980s. Appearance deceives. Thin, wiry creatures can be the most ruthless; they even attack when not provoked. Peligro. Danger. Not worth it.

Like the Burmese python she had seen in one abandoned neighborhood, she coiled herself around the chair, flexed herself. She felt the need to approach him. Saliva started to pool in her mouth, her quadriceps tightened with the need to spring and pounce.

She stopped herself just before leaping out the gate and pursuing him. Walking back to her chair, she sank down. In the distance, she saw live oak trees dripping with Spanish moss. Where were the alligators tonight? Were they in the mangrove swamps, or were they taking over the fountains and personal spas in abandoned neighborhoods? Cicadas buzzed.

She paid her bill and walked outside down a tropical rock garden. Something made her sniff the air, and what she sensed electrified her. Dial soap. Ben Gay.

The Praying Mantis man was nearby. Evidently, he was injured. He would absolutely be easy prey.

******

The newspaper vending machine in the entryway of the hotel displayed the front page of the local newspaper. It featured a picture of a Nile Monitor lizard with a chunk of flesh and what appeared to be poodle fur hanging from its thin lips.

Seven-Foot Lizard Preys Upon Pets

With a mouth full of kill, eyes glittering with satisfaction, the lizard looked absolutely at home in Florida.

In the moonlight, Tinguely's eyes shone.

If she had caught Praying Mantis man, what would she have done with him, anyway?

Dog Days

Love is the only sane and satisfactory answer to the problem of human existence.

Erich Fromm

She did it for love. She took the brick of mutilated, torn, weathered $100 bills to the bank to exchange it for a million or so bucks of fresh U.S. currency.

****

The white pit bull barked listlessly in the heat. She was used to holding forth from mowed grass and a Wet 'n Wild kiddie wading pool where her yardmate, a once-burly black German Shepherd named McCain, lay chin-deep, in the tepid water.

Late July. Dog days.

Tinguely Querer approached the white pit bull, whom she had dubbed Hillary. Hillary perked up to see Tinguely approach.

"I'm a real confidence booster for you, right?" Tinguely felt beads of sweat form on her back and roll slowly down. It was only 9:30 a.m. "You run up, bark, growl, and menace me with your sharp canines. It works, dear, doesn't it? I always go away."

Hillary's smooth white coat rippled as her chunky, thick muscles rippled underneath. Low growl, then barks. Tinguely considered it a conversational gambit.

"Yes, it's a boring, hot day. You should be liberated from that backyard. You could be doing such interesting things—"

The pit bull stared, then put her head down. She looked at her. The hackles on the back of her neck stood up. From his kiddie pool, the black German Shepherd whined and shifted his weight in the pool.

****

For the past few years, authorities say, he and his family have popped in and out of U.S. banks, looking to change about $20 million in buried treasure for clean cash. The money is always the same—decaying $100 bills from the 1970s and 1980s. It's the story that keeps changing:

- It was an inheritance.
- Somebody dug up a tree, and there it was.
- It was found in a suitcase buried in an alfalfa field.
- A relative found a treasure map.

So many things are simply a matter of point of view – in Veracruz, the Plaza of the Heroes commemorates the valiant defense by the Mexican naval forces against four different invasions.

Two were invasions by the U.S. – one in 1847 – during the Mexican-American War. That one did not surprise me.

The other invasion by the U.S. was in 1914.

1914??

That event never quite made it to the history books I studied in high school and college. It does not seem to make it to even the most politically inclusive undergraduate history texts (U.S. History after the Civil War). This I know because I've worked extensively in developing instructional materials – overviews, lectures, quizzes, and podcast scripts – for U.S. and world history textbooks.

I never saw any mention of the 1914 invasion by the U.S., although there is often mention of the U.S. military's meddling (or "helping") in political and economic affairs in Central America.

I will say that, if anything, the textbooks focus on the U.S. desire to maintain an isolationist stance during that time. However, I am not sure how that squares with the Spanish-American War (of 1898).

Times and attitudes change quickly, I suppose, and life in 1898 was different than U.S. daily life in 1914. Americans did not want to get into the "Great War" any more than they welcomed the enthusiastic rabble-rousers, Emma Goldman and other anarchists.

Americans defend life, liberty, and justice for all.

That's the goal, at least, and it's the utopian side of a coin with two faces.

Heads or tails? Liberators or invaders?

Which do you prefer?

Sunray, Texas

Flat, short-grass prairie. Vast sky. A line of massive wind turbines. I stop on the edge of the farm road that leads to them. Take photographs. The white turbines are breathtaking.

Resume my drive. In the distance, I see what appears to be a small housing community or subdivision. As I approach, I notice it is a feedlot – feed and piles of feed. The cattle are standing on mounds of feed. Many are shoulder to shoulder. There are five separate pens. I estimate that at least 2,000 head of cattle are distributed between the pens.

Silence.

No sign of people. The wind turbines move silently in the sky. The cattle groan. There is absolutely no traffic except for a white half-ton Ford pickup that passes me as I'm stopped on the edge of the asphalt, looking at a clutch of purple vetch.

The nearest farmhouse is at least five miles away. It also stands silently in the prairie, with no signs of human activity.

The wind blows. I catch a whiff of wet earth mixed with cattle.

The McDonald's near the state highway was filled with a couple of vanloads of three- or four-year-olds. Their mothers did not let them play on the equipment outside, perhaps because it was dark and the door to Playland was locked. Instead, they ran and squealed with tall cones of soft serve ice cream and whatever toy they were handing out in the Happy Meals. The mothers seemed indifferent, even oblivious.

The moms were probably abusing over-the-counter cough medicine, thought Tinguely. If she had her way, she'd create a bright, enticing piece of playground equipment that was, in reality, a cage. Lock them in. Let them out when they'd finished smearing their food in their smocks, t-shirts, and hair.

Win-win.

Tinguely was in no mood for win-win.

She wanted "win"—and did not care what the other party got, or if she ever had contact with anyone (the world) again. Today had been a ridiculously difficult travel day. She was not in the mood to bargain with God, the weather, fates, or some sort of food genie that would make tasty, affordable, and easy-to-carry food available at the airport. She would take what she could get, just so she was left in a position of being able to do what she was supposed to do. No time to haggle. The negotiating process was only fun when feeling powerful (or indifferent).

Dad asked her to go to Muleshoe, Texas to find out what was going on, and to make sure that they had finalized a couple of contracts. She did not have time to drive from where she was in Oklahoma. So, she decided to fly to Amarillo and then rent a car. She had to go. That was non-negotiable.

"I'd like you ask around and find out if there is any enhanced oil recovery—EOR—going on across the border in New Mexico," said Dad.

"How? Where?" asked Tinguely.

"There's an old field, which, according to my proprietary detection methods, is completely depleted. However, a company in Oklahoma City claims they've found a new way to use carbon dioxide injection for enhanced oil recovery," said Dad. "It's the Chavaroo field."

"Don't you mean Chavarro? There's no such thing as Chavaroo."

"West of Muleshoe there is. You're right, though. You'd think it would be 'Chavarro'—hmm," Dad paused. "Chavaroo—probably some sort of scrivener's error that became official. Some places have auspicious births. Others come into existence in a much more aleatory naming process."

"Yup, that's for sure," said Tinguely. "I've never heard you talk that way before, Dad. You're sounding almost like a lit geek."

"Bite your tongue," said Dad. "Then get your ticket lined up. We need to get after this. There could be some problems if that company out of Oklahoma City really is in the middle of our play."

"Are there lots of mules in Muleshoe?" asked Tinguely. She could not help laughing.

In point of fact, Muleshoe makes much of the fact that mules were used in ranching in the old XIT Ranch that covered much of the Texas Panhandle.

However, a mule shoe could also refer to drilling equipment used in deep, complex wells.

Mule Shoe (definition from oilgasglossary.com): Equipment used in drilling an oil well, a sub part of which is formed in the shape of a horseshoe and used to orient the drill stem downhole.

Any downhole muleshoes in Muleshoe? It was not likely—at least not the oil well kind. Oil was discovered in West Texas in the Yates Field. It is fairly close to Muleshoe. The oil and gas fields just across the border in New Mexico are of more interest.

****

It was the first day of spring. There was always a chance of violent weather, namely high winds, hail, and tornadoes.

Airlines, travelers, and businesses were trying to predict the impact, adjusting schedules, cutting their losses. A few were bargaining with Odin or Thor, while others simply looked at the situation with resignation.

"Dad. It looks bad. Say a prayer for me. Don't use the ones you might have used with the stock market or real estate. They didn't work."

"Okay, I will use the one I used to put up with the neighbor's dog."

Things you cannot change you cannot accept. That's really how it works.

Sure enough, they got bad weather—but it came in the form of freezing rain, at 4 a.m. just when Tinguely was leaving for the airport. To her surprise, the flight was not canceled. However, they did have to wait on the runway for an additional hour as the plane was de-iced—not once, but twice.

Once she got to Dallas, she found that her flight to Amarillo had been canceled. The Texas Panhandle had experienced a rare "thunder-snow" storm—they received five inches of snow, with violent winds, lightning, and thunder. The runway had drifts of snow which had to be cleared, but which kept blowing back thanks to the 40-miles-per-hour north wind.

Rebooked on a later flight, Tinguely noted with surprise that American Eagle had discontinued the regional jet service and no longer used the nice Brazilian Embraers. Instead, they had turboprop planes.

Thanks to the high winds, the flight was weight-restricted; they had to offer six passengers vouchers, hotel lodging, food, and guaranteed seats on the first flight the next day. Tinguely would have taken them up on it, but she had to drive to Muleshoe—apparently, in blowing, drifting snow, potentially even a whiteout.

If the going was tough for her, it would be equally tough for anyone else, reasoned Tinguely.

She took her place on the plane. As they took off, she noted that their cruising altitude would be 15,000 feet. That was a bad sign. It was likely to be a bumpy flight, thought Tinguely.

Bumpy never bothered Tinguely. The mild rocking, bucking, careening of the plane put her to sleep like a child in a car seat.

Other passengers were not so lucky. As she awakened at the end of the flight—which was about thirty minutes longer than in a regional jet—she noticed that a woman in her mid-fifties was using paper towels to mop up where the woman next to her had vomited on her. The airsick woman appeared to be in her late twenties with rather oily, curly brown hair. Three rows up, another person was either vomiting or combating hyperventilation in a plastic bag. Tinguely felt a sense of weird satisfaction and inwardly gloated that she felt fine. She knew she would pay for her *schadenfreude*, thanks to karma and the ineluctable ebbs and flows of good and bad vibes in the universe.

Predicting the behavior fluids and understanding the properties of rocks under pressure was suddenly important to people who lived and did business in, around, and under the surface of Muleshoe. Continuous Fracture Modeling (CFM) has been implemented in naturally fractured reservoirs west of Muleshoe. The idea is that mathematical modeling using neural networking with seismic and geomechanics data can better predict fluid behavior in the rocks. Does it really matter?

What happens when fluids hit particles, or vice versa?

Getting to Texas was not much different than getting to life's other various and sundry places. Things did not always go smoothly.

This was no exception. The car had a layer of snow on it, but no snow brush or ice scraper. It was 24 degrees, and Tinguely was forced to clear the snow the best she could—when she went back to the rental car kiosk to ask for a scraper (and to complain that the slacking Hertz employees were nowhere to be found), all the agent could do was give her a red plastic plate.

"Hey, that works!" she said, and used it to scoop off the remaining snow. As she made her way along the state highway, the low spots on the highway looked like Arizona arroyos in flash flood—but instead of water flowing across the washes and gullies, it was white, blowing snow. Underneath was water and ice, which made it treacherous. Thankfully, she only pseudo-donuted once. Others had not been so lucky. They were either in ditches or in the center median area.

On the way, she stopped for trail mix and to stretch her legs at a United supermarket. As she entered, she set off the anti-theft devices. The store manager ran up to her as the alarm bleated like a hyper-amplified ram caught in a cattle guard.

"I'm just coming in, not out. I'm not stealing anything."

"I'm sorry. I have to check out the situation when the alarm goes off. Company policy."

"This is embarrassing."

"Are you wearing anything from Old Navy?"

"No. I'm not wearing anything Army Surplus either. I got this jacket at Ann Taylor."

"New purse?"

"No."

Tinguely thought about her purse. Her black mock croc Brighton clutch did have some sort of barcode on a plastic strip inside the coin holder part of the clutch. She decided to pull it out—and stuck it to a bag of trail mix next to the one she picked up to purchase.

After she made her purchase, she left the store. Sure enough, the anti-theft detection devices did not go off. She was able to leave unmolested. The person who purchased the trail mix with the Brighton anti-theft barcode magnetic sticker on it would not be so lucky.

****

Muleshoe was directly north of the Permian Basin. It was northwest of fields in New Mexico. The Yates Field in the Permian Basin in southwest Texas is a naturally fractured reservoir that has good porosity through the fractures, along with natural vugs and dolomitized zones in the carbonate facies.

Things might be getting a bit better. Tinguely was able to admit a sliver of cautious optimism. On the other hand, she might still have some karma to work through. She really should not have felt *schadenfreude* at her fellow passengers on Flight Big-Barf.

Tinguely sighed and opened the bag of trail mix as she started her car. She munched on a handful of dried papaya, dates, walnuts, and almonds. Snow brought survival to mind. After surviving the winter by feasting on the flesh of their fellow travelers, did members of the Donner party ever have an appetite for fruit and nuts? Once you've literally eaten one of your own species, are you forever marked? What happens when another human's DNA and body fluids flow through your own veins, vugs, and volatility?

Tinguely was not given to motion sickness. On the other hand, she was very vulnerable to "concept sickness"—the idea of organ and bone harvesting always made her faint. Now, the idea of human competition to the point of cannibalism made her nauseous. She could not believe that when she was a child, she loved chocolate "gummi" candy in the shape and size of a house mouse, replete with a shiny pink tail.

****

As she pulled out of the United parking lot with her white Camry with only 300 miles on it, a police car followed her, its lights flashing to indicate that she should pull over.

A young policeman in a smartly-fitting navy blue uniform approached the car.

"Hello, officer. What did I do? I'm so sorry," said Tinguely. "I'm on my way to Muleshoe."

"Ma'am, do you realize your headlights were not on?" He took a look at her Oklahoma driver's license and her insurance card. "This could be a very dangerous situation."

"Oh, no. Wow, how weird—I thought they were on." Tinguely discovered she had not the slighted idea how to turn on the headlights on the Toyota Camry. In fact, she had assumed they were automatic.

Her luck was changing for the better. The officer instructed her how to turn on her lights, after she showed him the Hertz rental agreement, demonstrating she had only had the car a matter of hours.

Suddenly hungry, she pulled into the McDonald's for a chipotle snack wrap and a side salad. The floors were of polished fossiliferous limestone that had secondary calcitic cement in some of the vugs near the fossils. Most of the fossils were small—crinoid stems, brachiopods, mollusks, and a lone trilobite.

Actor Lee Horsley was born in Muleshoe on May 15, 1955.

He played the fictional detective, Matt Houston on an ABC series of the same name and later starred in the CBS western *Paradise*. Undoubtedly, he has had to put up with all kinds of cracks about his name and his birthplace (A Horsley born in Muleshoe? What is a self-respecting Horsley doing in Mule country, anyway?)

That's when the rugrats bearing soft serve cones raced toward her. Tinguely thought of a brigade of pugs dressed up for Halloween, scrambling after each other, racing toward the idea of something that made them frisk and bark.

Was it better to be a child than a dog? Better to be a dog than a Donner party survivor? Many thoughts raced through Tinguely's mind. Godzilla. It would be great to be Godzilla for an afternoon and stomp down the streets of a small, prosperous city and practice singeing cows, dogs, stray cats, and the occasional soccer mom with your fiery breath.

Was it better to be Godzilla or a soccer mom?

Such questions were delightful only when you were in the mood for indeterminacy.

Right now, anything particulate—children, dogs, grains of ice and snow, clumps of vomit—seemed determined to erupt, flow, get blown just where you wanted it least. That was the way of the world, at least on the surface.

You couldn't really say the same thing about the subsurface, especially in a naturally fractured, secondarily altered shoal facies carbonate.

Reality sometimes seemed infinitely negotiable.

Narratives of Maturation:
The Bildungsroman vs. Thermal Maturation of Hydrocarbons

How is the concept of thermal maturation of hydrocarbons in shales similar/not similar to the Bildungsroman?

Can the narrative employed to explain the process of thermal maturation, together with all its attendant assumptions, be applied to fiction? Or to biographical narratives?

It would be easy to say that this is simply an exercise in tracking analogies. I think that it can be more than that. What we can examine are the underlying assumptions that inform human maturation and geochemical maturation. We can also look at which we privilege – do we give preferential treatment to the process or the qualities that accompany each stage? What do we consider to be the triggering factors? What are the elements that are necessary for maturation? Because the Bildungsroman is such a well-known narrative form and such a well-trod genre, it is not a bad idea to start with the narrative of thermal maturation, in a rather skeletal form.

THERMAL MATURATION:

The "immature" state is a shale that contains a high carbon content. Kerogen is a mixture of organic chemical compounds that make up a portion of the organic matter in sedimentary rocks. Typically, it's an organic-rich shale. "Immature" signifies that the shale is in a relatively untransformed state. It is shale. Nothing has broken free from it – and the chemical that can eventually transform to hydrocarbon (methane to the more complex alkanes) has not yet undergone pyrolysis, etc.

VALUE JUDGMENT:

"Immature" is valueless, except in its function as a "seal" over a porous rock that functions as a sponge – it holds liquids (like oil) – thus creating a trap for the oil.

Process is everything, especially when it involves trial by fire: How does natural gas emerge from carbon-rich shale? The key is maturation. What kind of maturation? It's thermal. In other words, the temperatures must ascend to the point that the shale breaks down, physically and chemically – it starts to become more fissile, have fractures (which function as conduits for the newly formed gas). The shale starts to change chemically – the kerogen transforms and starts to break down. This sounds very straightforward until you realize that that triggering mechanism – heat flow – has to be at an ideal rate. Otherwise, metamorphosis takes place and the shale transforms into hard, non-hydrocarbon bearing metamorphic rock such as slate.

If the heat flow happens too quickly and intensely, any hydrocarbons that might have started to form combust. They burn off. They're simply gone.

If the heat flow is too mild and the rate of heating is too slow, there may be a bit of in-situ methane, but not in commercial quantities, and it will be hard to recover because it's possible that fractures did not form.

APPLICATION TO LITERARY NARRATIVES:

1. Maturation requires a triggering event, and the event is never pleasant.

2. Heat is part of the equation – not low heat or a fiery flashpoint sort of flameout. It takes time. It's slow-cooked. The heat is constant and lasts a long time.

3. Application of heat (discomfort) has to be constant and continuous. Episodic heat as well as episodic tectonic activity (movement of the earth) are necessary in order to liberate the gas and create rocks that have fractures through which the gas can move.

4. Too much or too little will result in a failure to mature correctly. Too much heat means a destruction of the organics, too little means that nothing happens – just a seemingly endless stasis. Paralysis – emotional, physical, psychological.

UNDERLYING PARALLELS:

The Bildungsroman looks ahead to the end-point – the making of the writer/artist, and at formative events, I guess we like to assume maturation is a process because it gives us hope.

We like to think that there are causes and effects. There are lessons learned. That's how we mature.

But is it?

How about the adults who seem to become less mature over time – which is to say that they seem to learn NOTHING from their bad experiences. In desperation, we call the behavior an "addiction" or a "compulsion."

I think it's sort of an anti-maturation narrative.

I'm going to give it a try. I'd like to experience anti-maturation myself (but not in a way that looks like addiction, compulsion, or gambling).

If you were to accidentally hit a small black bear on your way back from the lake, and hit it so hard with your truck that you were to kill it, would you take it back home for your dogs?

For my dogs? As a playmate?

No. As food.

Road kill?

Yes.

No, I would not. I would notify the State Conservation Commission.

****

"I'm rooting for the bears."

The radio talk show host was responding to a caller who was complaining that the government was not doing enough to protect people at national parks from bear attacks.

"You feed them, you taunt them, you learn a lesson," said the host. He was responding to the caller's suggestion to set out tranquilizer-laced bear food, and then catch and put them in compounds where tourists could take special tours.

"The tours could bring in a lot of money," said the caller.

The host was not polite to her.

"We learn lessons from the wild," he said. "What kind of lesson is it to simply pump pharmaceuticals down the throats of any living creature that doesn't act like a lawn flamingo or fancy living room accessory?"

The host was getting testy. The caller may not have known it, but she was in for an emotional cudgeling. It was what the host was famous for.

"I'm also in favor of flea and tick dips for the deer that could be potential carriers of Lyme disease," the caller said.

"We need to help them. Overpopulation is not easy."

"Ma'am. Do you mind me asking where you live?" asked the host. "Not that it matters. Lack of meaningful or appropriate predators is a problem everywhere."

"I live in upstate New York. We've turned the Albany Pine Bush Preserve into a place where humans and wildlife can coexist. Human and wild habitats are checkerboarded."

"I hate to tell you this, but you're sitting on a time bomb. Checkerboarding means that the predators can move around within the plots of land. The prey tend to be the species that can't move. Predators are mobile. Prey are trapped. Nice," said the host.

"Well, I have heard people say that it can cause outbreaks of avian flu," said the caller, hesitantly.

His voice was sarcastic. "Time for a commercial break."

The next caller would certainly pick up on the predator reintroduction theme. They would talk about wolves, foxes, mountain lions, and catamounts. They would not get around to rapists, pedophiles, serial killers, neighborhood thieves, and arsonists.

Tinguely Querer turned off the radio. She was a long way from the caller's land and thousands of miles from the verdant glades, dramatic limestone caves, and cliffside waterfalls of the Helderberg Escarpment of upstate New York. She was in a different kind of wildness. She was in the American West. Where she drove, the western plains still bore traces of massacres, cattle drives, and poor farming and irrigation techniques.

She stopped at a large chain bookstore at a college town in western Oklahoma just east of where Custer had slaughtered women and children at the Battle of the Washita. Today, the place of spilled blood was marked by a steel historical marker. The famous chain bookstore, serving famous chain coffee was an oasis where she could wire herself up on too-strong

caffe americano and a sugary, high-fat donut-type pastry with a vaguely European moniker.

It was a new strip mall on the edge of the prairie. Tinguely scanned the horizon. The sky was blue and seemingly endless. A herd of American bison pushed themselves up into the far southwest corner of the fenced field that bordered the bookstore parking lot. The dark brown bovines stared, shuffled, and groaned as customers made their way from their pickups, minivans, and fuel-efficient hybrid cars. Tinguely had never realized how large the bison's eyes were. They were black, rounded demitasse cups where you could see the sky and your soul reflected, only upside down.

"Room for cream?" asked the young woman at the coffee bar. She was wearing an "Ask About Our Book Club Member Discounts!" t-shirt, and a stack of application forms were perched next to the glass apothecary jar containing individually-wrapped amaretto biscotti.

"Do you still have free Wi-Fi?" she asked.

"No. It's five dollars for two hours. We had too many people who just sat here all day and looked at porn. The company tried to block it, but online predators are pretty skillful." The young woman appeared to be a student at the local college.

"You had pedophiles here? At this location?" Tinguely was amazed.

"No. It was a company-wide problem. So, they changed the policy."

Tinguely flipped open her laptop, paid the fee for two hours of Wi-Fi and started browsing the headlines. She was not in the mood to start working on the report her dad was expecting. Drilling activity in the Anadarko Basin had picked up, and the drilling, seismic, and service company crews were staying in hotels that had not seen occupancy rates like these since the oil boom of the late 70s and early 80s. The Indians and Pakistanis who had bought the bankrupt motels in the late

80s were finally going to see a payoff for all their work. They had kept the motels immaculate, although threadbare, counting razor-thin bars of soap and bleaching washcloths and towels already transparent from too many washings.

"Yeah, I was all for the bears, too," said a voice emanating from the other side of the bar. They were talking about football, not nature—at least not directly.

Tinguely Querer looked up from her laptop where she had been reading articles on maulings, freak accidents, and celebrity scandals from a BBC online news source. She liked the European perspective. Supposedly, big brown bears had gone killer in the Kamchatka Peninsula of far eastern Russia and were mauling employees of the local platinum mine.

A two-minute video newscast featured long panning shots of the massive forest, the taiga, and the gated entrance to the platinum mine.

"Two guards at the mine showed signs of having been gnawed on," said one mine employee. Her eyes were red and puffy from crying. She was speaking in Russian, and the English was dubbed over her voice.

The voices on the other side of the counter continued to discuss football and sports.

"The Bears are really aggressive this year. Not that it does them any good. They are doomed."

The platinum mine operator looked at the camera. The Kamchatka Peninusula was north of China, and officially a part of Siberia. It would be easy work to kill the guards, steal the platinum, and then mutilate the corpses so they looked as though they had been mauled by bears.

Winning is everything.

The Illusion of Time

They replayed the forty-yard pass oh I don't know how many times, and my mind, as it is, always scrimmaging, went a bit flat for a moment; they ran out of time, and well, the clock ticking and running out would be more unbearable than usual. It's because I wasn't expecting it. I was thinking we'd actually win this time. But maybe not. Who can say. Time was not on our side.

The latest SCIENTIFIC AMERICAN posits that time is a construct. Time (measurable, linear) does not exist. It's just a convenient organizing principle; a narrative form expressed in symbols and not with the kind of words we use to spin our fables and our admonitory tales.

I see it. My mind unfolds memories that I ply back and forth like a kayak on a small, rough mountain stream. With every move, I pay forward the emotion I will be compelled to feel. What do you think of that?

"We do not move from the past to the future, but from right to left, and then from left to right."

Objects in motion. The mind imposes a sequence, but only because we've trained ourselves to believe that the pattern is correct.

Can we reject time entirely? What do we do with all our theories and technologies that rely on time? There's Newtonian physics, mathematics, and of course, financial/ business math. Financial instruments are built on time. They are time constructs.

Are the ideas about the consistency/homogeneity of time just absolutely wrong?

You leave the office at 5 p.m.

I leave my office at 5 p.m.

We meet at a restaurant at 8 p.m. Is the time I've spent, since leaving the office, the same as the time you've spent? How about if your interval was filled with memory-making events that you'll revisit many times? What if mine was utterly forgettable; just traversing the same old, same old places, and doing the same thing I always do?

Timelike events: they seem to be causally related.

Spacelike events: They seem to be causally unrelated, but they take place in the same space.

Time is not a piece of us. We are a piece of time.

Time is an invented placeholder for the things we value.

Time is often not time at all, but a narrative disguised to look and act like what we want to believe is time.

Narratives masquerade as time.

Narratives foreground and yet also camouflage the effects we attribute to time.

Narratives are not time.

Time is something else.

* *

Time is money. How many times have I heard that? The way I spend my life has value; when I spend it doing something I dislike, then the chunk of life I've spent doing the thing I dislike suddenly has more value. Call it opportunity cost.

Search for the convenient explanations to illustrate the anxieties associated with the construct of time.

Money is a technology that leverages time. The problem with the economy today is that we need to innovate and improve our time technologies. We need to leverage time in new ways; invent instruments to give people the chance to build on time.

Technologies of time? Negotiable instruments to multiply money and capitalize projects.

* *

Tarnished time. Warped time.
Squeaky clean time.

All are the foundations of narratives.

* *

NARRATIVES OF ENERGY, TIME, TECHNOLOGIES:

Because the world tends to classify energy as "clean" or "dirty," and "good" or "bad," would it not follow that the narratives will only escalate over time? We'll have a good vs. evil narrative – a grand clash-of-titans showdown. At least that's what the narrative expectations would lead one to expect.

REAL-LIFE INTRUSION:

I'm in Starbucks right now and I'm amazed, as always, by the flow of crowds/customers. It's never an even stream. Either there is no line at all, or there is a long line. It's not just that people come in groups, it's that the groups cluster together. Five minutes ago, there was no waiting. There was no activity for five minutes. In the last thirty seconds, four groups (clusters of two or more) and three individuals came in, for a total of around a dozen people in line. It's pretty amazing. I'm also amazed at the range of apparel options. It was cold last night – 30 degrees or so – and today is sunny. It is supposed to reach 50. Most people are wearing long-sleeved shirts, pants, jackets, or hoodies. But here comes a guy in baggy shorts and a t-shirt. It's hard to understand! I wonder if crowd behavior is somehow determined by internal narratives; predictive of where people will be and when they should be there. There's an adorable pug sitting on a pile of dried oak leaves on the brick sidewalk. His leash is wrapped around a metal post, and he seems to be waiting quite patiently.

ILLUSION OF TIME AND NARRATIVE INEVITABILITY:

The more people classify items into good or bad, the more quickly they put themselves on a path to narrative inevitability.
"Narrative inevitability" has to do with a narrative that is so ingrained that if you have a story/tale/set of facts that gets anywhere close to it, the narrative will pull you in, drag you downstream, and right over the falls. Think of falling into the river that flows into Niagara Falls – that is the pull of narrative inevitability. The only way to avoid it is to try to make sure your set of facts do not start shaping themselves so that they fall right into the stream of narrative inevitability.

Somewhere along the line, it's important to start reshaping your story so that it fits a different, competing narrative that fits your needs and purposes a bit more clearly/ adeptly.

"What annoys me most about talk about space aliens is the idea that they are smarter, bolder, more technologically advanced than we are. Not to mention more ethical than earth-dwelling hominids, than us, the flat-footed mortals that we are." Tinguely Querer was talking to her father on her BlackBerry as she made her way to the Broken Bow Public Library.

"Uh—isn't that kind of obvious?" said her dad.

"What do you mean?" she said. She lost the signal before he could answer. It did not matter. She rarely paid attention to her father's opinions on such things.

Tinguely was approaching the outskirts of Broken Bow. The sky was pea-soup green, with golden edges around the horizon. With a flash, she realized it was tornado season. Not a good time to be traveling. In the copse of trees outside the city's edge, fireflies glowed and flickered. The hair on the back of her arm stood up.

Broken Bow was a part of the Arkoma Basin, and firmly in the midst of shale gas fever. This was an information session, and Tinguely's job was to find out the level of interest in the Fayetteville shale. She also needed to find out what people were saying. Were they unrealistic? Did they think that the Fayetteville would bring them the same sort of bonuses and royalties as the Barnett Shale play centered around the Dallas-Fort Worth airport?

She was supposed to talk about oil and gas, but reports of UFO sightings over the Beaver's Bend Resort and State Park had distracted her. Someone had reported Sasquatch and Bigfoot sightings as well as glowing lights and what appeared to be a quick-moving, saucer-shaped spaceship.

The olive-green sky and the utterly atmospheric stillness give her an otherworldly feeling. It was, objectively speaking, quite titillating. She had always like the idea of being abducted and probed by hyper-intelligent beings who might consider her a lab experiment for their highly-advanced doings. They had to be creatures of preternatural intelligence. Otherwise, she was vaguely revolted. Who wants to be poked, prodded, and otherwise investigated by a clod, a dolt, a lump—no matter how intriguing and alien their extraction?

"Is it true that an Apollo 14 astronaut saw the aliens?" asked Tinguely to a guy at the local McDonald's.

"Yes, ma'am. He also saw aliens during the mission. I read about it in last week's *Weekly World News*," he said.

"Hah. Proof positive NASA fed the astronauts hallucinogenic drugs so they'd think they had gone to the moon. They would even have tales to tell—I always thought the whole thing was a big farce," Tinguely said.

What was the purpose of such a production? It was hard to say. Sure, there were Cold War space-race competitions for hearts and minds. Tinguely thought it had to do with the Disneyfication of consciousness. The Disney version of reality is always better than the truth. The copy is more appealing than the original. Why? You can change it.

Disney is truth. It is an essential truth. Refined. Without the irregularities and scruffiness of the natural world.

Nice to know.

Just another paranormal scam. Tinguely was all too familiar with them. She remembered the time her sister had enlisted the help of a local television station's "The Real Ghostbusters" crew. They took photographs of the woods where their ancestor had supposedly hanged himself 250 years before. The photos were unremarkable except for a flock of what appeared to be fireflies glowing in the darkness. All would have been well if it had been July. It was, however, not July, but darkest November, just before the snow flew.

"Evidence—clear and true—of paranormal activity," said Tinguely's sister.

"Tell it to someone else," said Tinguely. If she couldn't turn it into a profitable, paying gig, she wasn't interested. Something, somewhere, was, somehow, watching her. It made her flesh creep.

The fact that several people had showed up at the local library helped settle Tinguely's nerves.

A woman wearing what Tinguely's mother used to call a muumuu cradled her teacup Chihuahua in her lap. The Chihuahua licked a worry spot on its left foreleg.

"I think there was a sighting." The woman spoke. The dog let out a yelp. "Otis! Hush."

NO SMOKING

NO PETS (includes snakes and ferrets)

"Mary Jo. Let's get back to the brass tacks. I'm not here to talk about space aliens. I want to talk about that Fayetteville shale gas play I keep reading about." Man in L.L. Bean shirt, khaki pants, and cowboy hat looked pointedly at Tinguely. "Are you going to tell us about the play? Can we lease our land?"

An intrusive thought pushed itself into Tinguely's mind. She wondered how the guy in the cowboy hat made love to his wife. Aggressive? Thrusting? Insensitive? That was what came to mind.

Tinguely shuddered. Time for deflection.

"Sir. Here is my card. Website address. I'm not really the decision-maker. I'd recommend emailing our land department."

The man took the card, thanked her, and read it closely.

Otis jumped to the carpet. He walked around in a circle, scuffing the floor with his hind feet. He sniffed and stole furtive glances. Then, abruptly, he squatted on his haunches.

"Otis!"

"Ma'am. Your dog just, uh, pooed on the library carpet."

Mary Jo lumbered toward the ladies room to get paper towels and liquid hand soap. Her muumuu made a rustling noise, her plastic bracelets clattered.

Tinguely used the distraction to her advantage.

"What makes you think that aliens prefer Broken Bow?"

"Who knows. They're smarter than we are," said the guy in the cowboy hat. "Advanced technology. They can take over us whenever they want. Some people say they already have. They live among us."

Tinguely looked at him.

"With all due respect, sir, I don't agree. I maintain that aliens are remarkably stupid. But, like sharks and cockroaches, they have a knack for surviving even the most hard-hitting mass extinction event."

"So—what about the Nazca lines? The pyramids? The Mayan ruins? You think these were made by people and not aliens?"

"I think that believing in aliens is a great way to start a religion or provide justification for a space program," said Tinguely. "In reality, I think they just happen to visit our planet along with others—we have tasty snacks they like."

Mary Jo returned to the room. She picked up Otis's leavings with a paper towel. "Snacks? What do you mean?"

"I think she means that the space aliens would like to snack on Otis if they could get a chance to do so," said Cowboy Hat, smiling.

Tinguely's mother's words echoed in her ears: "I'm going to tell myself I like eating and that I have an appetite."

Tinguely's mom was skinny. She liked to pretend that she was trying to gain weight. It was a ploy to draw attention to her thinness. At least that was what Tinguely believed. Tinguely secretly hated her bragging and gloating about her thinness.

"Well, Mom. Lucky you. I have a huge appetite and my only way of monitoring and controlling myself is to keep all food, alcohol, and credit cards (for online purchases) far from me."

Tinguely paused. At least she had managed to avoid an addiction to pornography and online gambling. It was simply through the grace of God that she had not developed those compulsions, she thought.

Mary Jo adjusted her muumuu. She was surprisingly attractive for a woman of her heft. Not a single wrinkle, observed Tinguely.

"You're saying that space aliens might eat dogs?" Mary Jo smiled.

"I don't think so. I think they eat radiation. Maybe the tops of trees. But only for the photosynthesis." Tinguely paused. "But, what do I know?"

Cowboy Hat smiled, "What do any of us know about that? I am more interested in leasing my land and getting a well drilled. I need some cash flow so I can put in a new barn. I am also thinking about raising all-natural poultry. I want my turkeys and chickens raised free-range, without antibiotics."

Mary Jo picked up Otis. She looked at Cowboy Hat. "Can I get a ride with you?"

After they left, Tinguely walked slowly to her car. She craved ice cream. Her mother's voice intruded: "Just tell yourself you have a normal appetite."

"Mother, I would prefer to be honest and face the truth. I don't know how or why mind games I might play with myself could possibly work. I mean, am I not aware of my own thoughts?" Tinguely hated cognitive dissonance.

Playing mind games with oneself—and losing—was all a part of the dumbing down of consciousness. After a while, people deny and disown their own honest perceptions.

No wonder people thought space aliens were more intelligent than humans.

I'd like to have a nice, long talk to figure out what went wrong (and what goes right). But we'd probably go in circles. At least, that's what I do. I approach the truth, or at least an essential, unchanging element, and suddenly, I'm a bead of mercury and I deflect myself, or I shatter into a thousand tiny globules.

Eventually, I reconverge with my brother and sister globules, and I'm a big bead again – with just a small film of dust on the top.

It's surprising how we used to play with mercury. My mother disinfected my wounds with white merthiolate – it did not sting like the red stuff. Both had a base of mercury. I scraped myself often in those barefoot summers of running across lawns, down the street, and into the neighbors' splash ponds, fountains, and pools.

The Old XIT Cattle and Social Club

The Old XIT (pronounced "excite") Cattle and Social Club was meeting in a small town southwest of the small town of Cactus, Texas.

Tinguely Querer looked at the announcement in the local paper and wondered what that the members of the club did for fun. Bingo? Monopoly? Horseshoes behind the barn? Knife throwing?

She wondered what it would take to join, and if it would be okay to join and attend just one meeting.

It was hard to predict when she would be in the Texas Panhandle and precisely where she'd be. After all, the Panhandle was a large place, the same size as eight Rhode Islands.

****

Back home in Oklahoma, she shared her thoughts with her mother.

"I would never join a Cattle and Social Club," said Tinguely. "Out of principle. I don't think that animals that are about to be slaughtered have much in common with people looking for love."

"Oh, you don't, do you?" Tinguely's mother had reappeared after a long absence. Once back in town, she gave Tinguely a call, and they met at the local Starbucks. Mother drank a green tea frappuccino. Tinguely had a nonfat chai latte. Tinguely munched on granola and a wholegrain roll with maple almond butter while Mother feigned maternal concern.

Tinguely was not buying the maternal concern routine. There were too many episodes in the past, too much abandonment— not intentional, but in pursuit of a higher truth. Abandonment of one's children and pets was not an easy thing to confront, so

Mother had learned the art of deflection and rationalization. She also told some whoppers of tall tales.

The latest was when Mother told Tinguely she was on a cruise, when in reality, Mother was at a Christian version of a Hindu Ashram in northeast New Mexico where she went on a retreat with her Bible study group that focused on healing and praise.

When Tinguely learned that part of the retreat involved locking each individual in an isolation chamber, she was horrified. The women stayed for three days and three nights and logged their thoughts, visions, and hallucinations in notebooks with waterproof pages. All Tinguely could think of was the medieval diarist and mystic, Margery Kempe, who chronicled her pilgrimage to the Holy Land. If one read between the lines, one could see that Margery had to have been an absolute pain to travel with. Her visions tended to portend great calamity and personal discomfort. Mother tended to have similar visions— crashing planes, danger on certain routes, food contamination, evil spirit-infested hotels, and horribly aching feet riddled with corns, bunions, and blisters.

"Mother." Awkward pause. "It's nice to see you." Tinguely tried to keep her face expressionless. She did not want to give Mother an entrée into her private life, or an opportunity to express opinions about Tinguely's weight, hair, and clothes.

Mother could be scary-skinny, and she could be the kind of person you'd see on the first row of an Armani style show or in a PRAISE NOW televangelist ministry broadcast. Mother was a true believer.

One would think that being in faith-healing circles would give Mother a positive "I believe in miracles" outlook on life. It did, but it also engendered a deep cynicism about human nature as it existed in its unmediated "fallen" state.

"Don't you think that they're just looking for trouble? After all, both end up in the same place. The only difference is

BULL-
FIGHTING
FOR
BEGINNERS

in how they grind the flesh, and who consumes whom. That's why I'm a vegetarian."

"And why you've never remarried," added Tinguely.

"Well, my point, Tinguely, is this question: Don't you think the whole endeavor is fraught with a morbid fascination with hopelessness?"

"No, Mother, I don't. I think that the cattle are hanging onto life. All they want to do is breed in hopes of cheating death. That's not hopeless."

"I think you're giving those randy steers a lot of credit, dear," said Mother.

"Maybe," said Tinguely. She continued. "But Mother, let's look at the other side. The Social Club side. People looking for love are something else entirely. Renunciation of the individual self. At least that's how South Americans put it. If you renounce your individual sense of self, aren't you essentially obliterating yourself? Your identity?"

"You've put your finger on the slaughterhouse connection, Tinguely," said Mother. "Feedlot cattle. Sad men and women willing to erase themselves if only … well, if only they can feel love—even if only for a moment."

"Mother. That idea makes me want to weep. It's almost saying that the human condition is worse than that of doomed, soon-to-be-slaughtered cattle. People are willing to 'self-slaughter' if they can have a moment—no matter how fleeting—where they feel a warm, loving embrace—an existential acceptance that is, well, unconditional."

"I don't know if I'd go that far. Let's just say that the core 'pivot point' of existence—for cattle—for human beings—revolves around sex-death equations followed closely by an 'if I die, you'll love me more, and then you'll take my energy to build a huge, better world' equation. I don't think it's very healthy, Tinguely."

"What's it like to be in an isolation chamber for three days and three nights?" asked Tinguely, suddenly bold. She never knew Mother to have such insight into the human condition.

"I slept a lot," said Mother.

Some things would never change.

****

A couple of weeks later, Tinguely found herself in a small town southwest of the small town of Cactus, Texas, still curious about the XIT Cattle and Social Club.

She went to her first meeting, which was in an old rock-and-mortar building perched on the side of a steep hill that overlooked a small canyon. They sat on the patio, which was draped with strands of all-white Christmas lights. The air smelled of sage and rain.

"We were going to have square-dancing lessons, but our instructor called in sick," said a woman in her late twenties who was dressed in a gingham prairie dress.

Tinguely thought she looked like a grad student in anthropology or an escapee from an isolationist polygamous cult. Tinguely's first impression did not lead her astray.

"Hi. I'm Katwell Dantzen. I'm getting a master's degree in ethnology, and I'm doing my thesis on folk dances. I am really sorry we aren't having square dancing. I was really looking forward to it," she said. She extended her hand. "Are you new?"

"Uh. To this, I am," said Tinguely. "Where are the cattle?"

"The cattle are not actually invited. We just talk cattle when we can't talk about love," said a husky man with a kind face. "I'm Roy Anguster."

"So that means that pretty much all we talk about is cattle. Deworming, growth hormones, antibiotics, putting the weight on quickly and safely," said another man, leaner, with bushy white hair. He had a slightly less pleasant expression on his face.

Tinguely guessed he was embittered by the constant cattle talk. Love would spice it up a bit. As would square dancing.

"Say, Katwell, don't you know some moves? You're getting an advanced degree in this stuff, after all. You even have the costume for it. Even though I've never seen a lady wear cowboy boots with a long prairie-girl dress," said Roy.

The white-haired man with the slightly embittered face answered his BlackBerry.

"Hello. Hello? Can you hear me now? Bad signal. What? I'm not anywhere. I am just down here at the Cattle Club."

Katwell was talking to Roy about why she mixed boots with skirts. Tinguely tittered lightly to herself, unable to keep back the chuckles.

The man's face clouded as he continued to speak on his BlackBerry.

"No one. It's just the same old Cattle Club. Same as ever. Who am I with? Cattle Club. I'll be okay. Don't worry about me. Woops. Bad signal. You're cutting out. I'll call you when I get in."

"Your voice sounded really guilty just then," pointed out Tinguely.

The guy smiled. His face softened and he seemed approachable, suddenly.

"That was my daughter. She doesn't trust me a lick. Don't know why that is. She always thinks I'm on the verge of getting corralled by some woman who is up to no good."

"How do you know that isn't the case?" asked Tinguely. "Maybe you are." She smiled. This was fun.

"She doesn't know it, but I make myself sound guilty on purpose. It drives her crazy," he said.

"Kind of serves her right, doesn't it," said Tinguely.

"Give a person enough rope and enough time, and they'll

tie themselves the fanciest noose you'll ever see," smiled the man. "By the way, I'm Potter."

"As in Harry Potter?" asked Tinguely.

"Close. Potter Harris," he said.

Tinguely smiled. Images of cattle being levitated, flying on broomsticks, and goose-stepping while mooing in unison along a line of giant wind turbines flooded her mind.

"Looks like the place is shutting down for the evening." A woman was turning off the Christmas lights, shutting the doors.

"Will you be back next week?" asked Potter.

Roy and Katwell chimed in, "Hope to see you again sometime, Tinguely."

"Maybe. I never know. I'm always in different places, it seems," said Tinguely.

****

"They didn't talk about love, and they didn't really even talk about cattle," said Tinguely to Mother. She was able to get a good signal, so she had called her mother's home phone. Surprisingly, Mother had picked up.

"Will you go back?" asked Mother.

"They did not really do anything. All they really did was talk about what they might have done, but couldn't do. That was the square dancing."

"Sounds like a normal sort of meeting to me. Isn't that the way people really communicate? They hardly ever get around to being direct and asking for and getting what they really want."

Tinguely reflected for a moment.

"Who knows what he or she really wants anyway?" she asked Mother.

"Maybe that's why it's so much easier to give people what they demand, rather than demanding something yourself," said Mother. Her voice was starting to break up.

"Too much effort," said Tinguely. "Well, have to go now, Mother."

She ended the call, then called to the front desk of the hotel where she was staying to request another set of bath soaps, and then to complain that the wireless Internet signal was low, and that they had given her a handicapped room instead of a normal one. She always ran into or tripped on the fold-down shower seats. They always seemed to have mildew on them. Who designed these things anyway? Who actually thought about thinking from the handicapped person's point of view?

The woman at the front desk dealt with Tinguely's complaints with good humor. "Guess you got lucky this time," she said.

"Yes, if my luck continues to hold, maybe we'll run out of hot water, or I'll cut myself shaving my legs," said Tinguely. How did a person who was partially paralyzed or with mobility problems shave her legs?

Getting access. A handicapped person was basically all about positive self-actualization. They thought about how they could gain access and mobility.

The non-handicapped person's perspective: Losing access. Losing contact. Losing hope of transformative action.

The XIT Cattle and Social Club held the answers, and Tinguely sensed it. She just wasn't sure if she had the courage to find out.

Tinguely Querer found herself in Rattlesnake Bluff, Texas wondering, rather vacantly, if she had been a sex worker in a previous lifetime.

Not a geisha, not a courtesan, not a prostitute in a brothel, not sold as a child by an evil aunt to a pedophile, but something more akin to a roaming free agent—a teenager in linen as blue-gray as the Icelandic skies; a young woman in silks from Kyoto or from the Maiden's Tower on the edge of the Caspian Sea; a free-range heirloom chicken, with bright eyes, flashy beak, and showy, brilliant plumage.

Of course, in the end, free-range heirloom chickens are killed and eaten.

A big gray jackrabbit, with long ears and slim legs, bounded across the road to the largely dried-up lake. There was a rest stop on the way, with fountains, walking paths, and lovely vistas of an arroyo lined with cholla cactus and prickly pear. She could hear the faint buzz of a rattlesnake, but it was far enough away that she did not feel alarm, simply awareness.

*****

Abelard Tavollio joined the flagellant cult after he lost his wife to the Black Death. He took his scourge, bent the spikes inward, and mortified his back, chest, sides, and legs until thin strips of skin and splatters of blood festooned the walls. Blood flowed and clotted. In the next room, a fellow flagellant howled and chattered in an alien tongue. When Abelard heard that, he wondered if they had succeeded—if they had brought about the end of the world, and if the New Heaven and the New Earth would soon follow.

When he regained consciousness, he was stuck fast to the

old, fallen world. Abelard's wife was still in some unknowable place—a place without a name—hauled off by the death cart to some anonymous burial pit that would never appear on a map or in any churchyard registry.

As he blotted the clots and chunks of skin with a rag dipped in old wine and vinegar, tears streamed down his face. He rinsed his scourge in hot water, unfastened the spikes, and threw them into a corner. He fashioned the leather thongs into a braid, which he then interwove with flowers plucked from the garden under the anteroom windows. Carving her name into the handle, he plunged it into a sheltered place in the garden, next to a stone retaining wall and an apple tree laden with small green fruit.

*****

The man she had been searching for all her life drove up into the parking lot, his thin, tanned arm resting on the edge of the open window. She thought of Camelot, of sheath dresses, and flats with small leather bows on the toes.

*****

The crack-addicted pop star broke the glass containing Chivas on the rocks and carved the name of the love of her life onto her stomach. The reporter who had been interviewing her had to leave the room. She tended to faint at the sight of blood.

"My lover! My love!" sang the pop star as she traced the edges of the letters with the tip of a finger stained black.

When the reporter returned, the pop star laughed. Her voice had a serrated edge. "It was only a scratch."

After the love of her life was jailed, the tabloids often ran photos of the ragged highways the pop star had cut deep into her arm.

"I cut where he used to touch me," she said. At the same time, she was listening to a crackly, scratched vinyl playing the 60s girl group song, "He Hit Me (And It Felt Like a Kiss)."

*****

Tinguely Querer's BlackBerry had stopped working at a place about fifty miles from Rattlesnake Bluff where a long line of high-tech wind generators shadowed old windmills pulling water from the Ogallala aquifer.

She could not check her stocks, the day's headlines, or her email. The worst part of it all was that she was not able to stream the Tech-Trance station she listened to as she drove across the high plains, the chaparral, and as she walked down into the canyon to check on the old pumping units and gas compressors to see which ones should be plugged, their pipe and casing pulled and cannibalized for newer, fresher production.

Without her BlackBerry and music from the Internet, she had to manufacture her own music. After all, if she did not dance—at least inside—her heart would stop beating. The beat, the images, the songs were her heart. Echoes of the Silk Road and a small caravanserai rang on the rocks. Hoofbeats from Chingiz and the Mongols outside a sultan's palace in Sheki in old Azerbaijan flooded her ears.

Taking down notes, manually calculating the GPS coordinates of the equipment, Tinguely looked up the side of the bluff. A small black-spotted lizard darted across the weathered limestone.

The warm canyon wind caressed her arms, and it felt like music.

When she inhaled deeply, the sage and ozone from a thunderstorm in the distance filled her. Echoes, shadows, mirages.

A cloud passed between Tinguely and the sun. She should be punished for pleasure. The sun reemerged. She should be rewarded for pleasure. She should dance, and dance as she saw fit, across lifetimes.

***

When his self-inflicted wounds finally healed, his wife came to him in a dream. "I'm going to whip some sense into you," the dream wife said. He flinched. The spikes were still in the corner in a small, bloodstained heap.

His wife laughed. "I knew you'd take it literally."

She stood over him, stroked his reddish and pink scars. "Stop hurting yourself. The end of the world already came and went. It left you behind. So, whether you're in heaven or hell does not matter. I am with you."

When he awoke, he knew just where the death cart had hauled her body, and where it lay. It was on the edge of a small orchard where someone had planted peaches from the stones carried in a pouch from southern Persia.

***

The man she had been searching for all her life walked slowly to her car. His face carried the warmth of years of summer sun. He held a bottle of Coke in one hand, a book of poetry in the other.

"I have the sense we may not have much time together," he said. "We must bear that in mind."

She did not hear him. The music from his car stereo was making her heart pound, her mind's eye moved into different directions.

"I have something to give you," he said.

She looked at him and took the book of poems he offered her. The BlackBerry in her field pack started working again. The GPS automatically registered their coordinates.

Big Big Sky

Saw antelope today and a wild songbird smashed on the front headlight of a rented Impala. "Aren't you going to clean it off?" I asked. The day after Memorial Day and it seemed especially grisly. "I am not touching it." That's what he said.

Well. Speechless.

Sent via BlackBerry from T-Mobile

* * * * * * * * * *

The antelope were in a field adjacent to a big, new wind farm they're putting in just south of Elk City, Texas. They were not actually smashed onto the front headlight of a rented Impala, although the text message made it seem that way. Antelope Meets Impala. Boy Meets Girl.

The little bird did really hit the car. It was stuck in the headlamp, its little beak half open. "I didn't do it on purpose," said the guy who had rented the car. He was eating a soft serve ice cream. An image of him zooming from one side of the road to the other, just trying to hit a bird flashed into my mind. I wonder how many squirrels he had run down in his life. Probably not too many. He does not own a car, he says. He just rents them.

It was very sad. I could not help but think of the two birds that kept chirping at me as I ran laps on the little asphalt track in the back of the Window on the Plains Museum, located on the south edge of town off Highway 287, the main throughfare linking Denver and Fort Worth via

Amarillo. The grassy area was an outdoor exhibit for old farm implements and oil and gas equipment. I think that the birds must have had a nest in the prairie grass because every time I got near, they started flying toward me and squawking so loudly I could hear it through my iPod earbuds.

You'd think he'd at least clean the bird's body and feathers out. Dignity. What ever happened to that? Who drives around with an animal or bird carcass like a hood ornament???

"It is going to start to smell," I pointed out. If you ran over a dog, would you just keep it stuck to your fender?

The famous WWII photograph of the desiccated head of a soldier who died fighting Rommel in North Africa went through my mind. It was still in the tank where he died. I always hated that photograph. It seemed to me that it stripped the poor man of his dignity. You can't just let their bodies hang out there in public. What was the name of the poor woman who drowned in New Orleans, whose body lay on the street for days? What have we come to if we do not treat our dead (even animals) with loving kindness?

I looked at him as he ate his ice cream and realized that my way of thinking was utterly alien to him.

"Yeah, avian flu. I don't blame you," I said. What else was there to say?

* * * * * * * * * * * * * * * * *

The Elk City cemetery had clearly been visited on Memorial Day. Flowers, ribbons, sprays, wreaths were there in abundance. The air still smelled a bit of rain and mud from the storms that had passed through a few days before. I noticed that not all headstones shared in such bounty. People die, relatives move away, and it's hard to find time to go and pay one's respects. My grandmother is buried in the Ardmore, Oklahoma cemetery just south of the Arbuckle Mountains on the highway to Lake Murray. I believe it is called the Rose Hill cemetery. I need to go and pay my respects soon. This year, it will be forty years since she passed away. I still remember that her birthday was in June. She was from Texas. Her last name was McLean, the same name as a town just east of here. Her mother's last name was Potter. Potter County is the county just west of here. The coincidences make me mindful of my grandmother whenever I'm in the Texas Panhandle. The power of naming is hard to overstate.

My grandmother used to tell me I was lucky I had a round face because I would not have wrinkles.

Why do we pay respects to the dead? It's hard to say. I think that on some level, we believe that the dead are still with us. Of course, they are - in the sense that they influence mental activity. The images in our brains could, in theory, be recorded, captured, and then projected like some sort of holograph into the world. And, we remember them.

Will the spirits of the dead come back to haunt us if we do not treat them well? I guess it depends on how they died. If it's a suicide, the survivors feel helpless and angry. In a certain way, the spirits of the living haunt the legacy of the dead, since the fact of suicide seems to cloud everything else.

I was perusing the NORTON ANTHOLOGY OF POETRY this afternoon and skimming through the biographical sketches. It was amazing how many poets were listed as having committed suicide. That's a heck of a thing, isn't it - you get fifty words or perhaps seventy-five, if you're a big deal. If you committed suicide, twenty of the words could be dedicated to describing your ignominious end. Dismal! Sylvia Plath, Charlotte Mew, John Berryman, Anne Sexton - these were just a few.

Why do we pay respects to the dead? Just in case their

spirits to walk the earth, you might as well get them on your side. You might need them to go junk yard dog on the people who seek to harm you. What that means in practical terms is that I need to learn how to think on my feet.

Then I can run or fly away.

It is better than being turned into a hood ornament.

The server in this restaurant is talking about her leopard gecko that was eaten by her cat.

"I named it 'Pepper Pot' – it was sad, but it wasn't my fault," she said. The poor gecko was doomed by the name. Who would name a lizard after a soup – unless you intended it to be one of the ingredients?

I wonder if the cat got sick from eating a lizard. Cats are so finicky. I'm surprised the cat actually ate it. I would be less surprised if the cat killed the poor lizard and then just threw it over to the side to let it slowly desiccate in the sun.

I am not sure if I can believe anything that the members of the waitstaff are saying. One just tried to convince his co-workers that Britney Spears' "Oops I Did It Again" is a cover of a Louie Armstrong jazz song.

The idea is, well, not completely unbelievable. After all, DeadMau5 did an absolutely transcendent trance/electronica dance mix that was styled on a ballad that was just boring beyond words. I am in the mood to second-guess myself. Was it always such a great idea to insist on going it alone?

I have had opportunities to backpedal and do a low-key or part-time job ... accept a proposal of marriage ... well, I'm sure it wasn't really a bona fide offer. Just some sort of emotional gesture designed to curry favor – the warmth would wear off quite quickly, if it ever even made it that far after I called the bluff.

CALLING ONE'S BLUFF. I think that's what the Tea Party is going to be faced with. If they're really elected, their bluffs will be called. Are they really willing to dismantle government instead of enjoying the spoils of elected officialdom? Can they resist being co-opted? I have my doubts. It's better not to put people in positions where you call their bluffs. No one likes what they see. What if I had accepted the marriage proposal? Called the bluff? My opinion? No marriage. Just a big row – on some sort of ridiculous pretext – pick a fight, recant, refuse to honor the proposal. Say things have changed.

Blame it on the other person's "secret" – some essential thing they've been hiding, keeping under wraps until now. Now it's a deal breaker. What "it" is does not matter. What matters is that it's impossible to describe or define "it."

Take the Tea Party. Let's say they're elected. How do they save face when their bluff has been called?

It's simple. Just find someone to lay blame upon.

"I want to do all the things I promised in my campaign, but I can't and it's not my fault. It turns out that Washington is a tougher, harder nut to crack than I thought. There are things you would not understand. The situation is complicated. I can't really go into detail. It is just that it's not what it seemed. So. The deal is off."

Honestly, can't you just hear a newly-elected Tea Party person saying this – ways to rationalize that once they got to Washington, the big machine made it impossible to go about developing or maintaining a vision that was at all sustainable (and not simply a self-serving set of jingoistic statements that masquerade as profound ideology).

For the record, I sort of like the Tea Party. And they make a convenient case study. "The cat ate my gecko." It's sad. For some people (rather cruel and insensitive), it's tragicomic.

I had something special, but it was eaten by my emotional proxy, my pet, my cat.

Tinguely Querer emerged from the racquet club damp with sweat and ready to make the long drive across the dark city to her midtown apartment where she planned to take a hot shower and to collapse into a soft bed with clean cotton sheets.

It was not to be.

As she approached her car, parked under a light and in view of the surveillance camera, she saw the right rear end resting on the ground. Someone had stolen her right rear wheel. Not the tire, but the entire wheel. There was a small pile of five lug nuts on the ground.

It was the second time in two weeks that it had happened. The first time, Tinguely had interrupted the thieves, who sped off in a souped-up box of a car—an Element or something like it—that sounded like a Harley Davidson with glasspacks. She did not realize what had been happening until the wheel started to come off as she drove down the road, heading toward Starbucks.

"At least the wheel did not come off while I was on the turnpike or in traffic," she said to the tow truck driver.

They stole her wheel sometime before 9:15 at night on the shortest, darkest day of the year, which happened to coincide this year with a full eclipse of the moon, slated for around midnight.

"You were right," Tinguely texted her hairstylist, who had become a *soi-disant* mystic with tarot cards and psychic visions. She wasn't alone. Others were feeling the psychic groundswell, as late-night *Coast to Coast AM* interview subjects waxed eloquent on underground civilizations, reptilian aliens, Trilateral Commission meetings, Bohemian Grove, and 2012.

The eternal return of the apocalyptic narrative.

In the QuikTrip convenience store where Tinguely bought a coffee after airing up the spare tire, she noticed a bleached blonde woman with a chipmunk-like laugh that was so loud it echoed off the glass doors of the refrigerated SmartWater and sugar-free energy drinks. The woman was young, but with a laugh like that—the result of being goofed up on whatever cheap stimulant was available (meth? glue? shoe polish?)—she would be wizened and toothless within three years. She could run around the trees with the other toothless chipmunks on crystal meth, thought Tinguely. Ordinarily, Tinguely felt a twinge of compassion for the drug abusers who seemed to gravitate to the convenience stores. Tonight, though, after having her wheel stolen, Tinguely felt hostility, raw aggression.

"I wonder how much they got for my wheel," mused Tinguely. How long would it keep them high? They need to switch over to huffing gasoline. It's cheap.

"Except they probably did it partially for the thrill," commented Tinguely to no one in particular.

Someone was speaking Mexican-accented Spanish in a squeaky baby voice that someone had probably told her was "perky" and not simply annoying. She was showing her friend an engagement ring.

Tinguely paused by the door and punched the number in on her new iPhone, which had a finicky touchscreen.

"You seem grumpy," commented her friend. She knew it was pointless to call him since he was around 150 miles southeast of the racquet club, but she did.

"I am grumpy," said Tinguely. "I should be grateful. I know that. At least they took the whole wheel, and just one. It's better than having it fall off at sixty miles per hour."

Tinguely walked across the parking lot, and the sound of chipmunk laughter bounced up and down. Tinguely felt like turning around and running up to the chipmunk woman, recording her laugh, and uploading it to iTunes.

That laugh would be perfect for horror films. You could play the laughter just before the knife came down in the shower or the chainsaw appeared in Lovers Lane.

****

Tinguely walked through the door and opened her mail. She noticed a holiday card from the stock transfer company that had escheated 90,000 shares of stock she had inherited from her mother. The stock transfer company claimed they had tried to establish contact with her. Unfortunately, the stock transfer company tended to deluge everyone on their mailing lists with spam and junk paper mail, to the point that whenever she saw an envelope with their return address, she expected a sales pitch for unneeded (but very expensive) workshops and third-party goods and services—insurance, travel deals, even cosmetic surgery.

So, she didn't open her mail from them. She did not know she was not in contact. As a result, she was turned over to the State of Colorado.

Getting her stock back once it had been escheated—basically seized—by the State of Colorado was harder than Tinguely ever imagined

Now she was opening her holiday card.

It was a cute pop-up of gift boxes—blue and purple. Undoubtedly, someone had thought they were nice little Hanukkah or Christmas gifts.

Pandora's boxes, thought Tinguely.

Beware the gifts proffered by a securities transfer company. Not Trojan horses, but worse. Open the box, open the present, and unleash pesky, needling, *schadenfreude*-ish energies of the night.

Was it the kind of energy that drove people to steal a wheel from a car in a racquet club parking lot? Did someone know she was inside, playing tennis on an indoor court?

"Doesn't your current boss live down the street from the racquet club?" asked her friend. "Doesn't he have a sixteen-year-old who just got a small SUV?"

"That looks like an Element?" responded Tinguely. She paused. "Yes."

Her friend sighed loudly. Tinguely spoke.

"I wasn't taking it personally until now," she said. "I guess I should. The police seemed to think it was an unusual event and that no one wants Subaru tires and wheels. If I had a Ferrari, yes. A six-year-old Subaru? No."

She picked up the pop-up holiday card and peered inside the little pop-up boxes. Did they have gifts inside? The card was not elaborate enough for that. Revenge fantasies flowed through Tinguely's mind. How could she entrap the wheel thieves? It was not worth it.

Switching gears, Tinguely thought that the answers to the "big questions" were patently self-evident.

Therefore, they were not too interesting. She was more interested in the "nano-questions"—the subtle questions that left no "psychic footprint" to disrupt the flow....

"Morality does not unfold in a linear way," commented Tinguely.

She assumed the thieves were young, male, with beliefs of impunity and immortality.

How about cornered rats? Desperate, angry, unwilling to conform?

Time for a few rat traps, of the human type, thought Tinguely.

And, well, rats came in all ages, sizes.

It was sad.

Happy New Year.

Tinguely Querer left behind her favorite pair of jeans.

They were her favorites not because of cut or price or brand, but simply because they were a full two sizes smaller than the jeans she wore a year ago. Granted, the larger ones were always a bit too large, and the big ones were worn at a time when Tinguely was living in a basement apartment that lacked any sort of mirror except for the mirror on the mounted medicine chest in the one bathroom that had a one-piece walk-in shower.

As noisy, moldy, and spartan as it was, Tinguely missed the place. It was confidence-boosting to never quite have any idea of just how baggy and unflattering one's jeans might be, and just how and why wearing dress jackets a couple of sizes too large leads to uncomfortable cognitive dissonance in the eye of the beholder.

Of course, you don't know that if you don't have a mirror.

You don't know how much weight you've lost if you don't have any scales.

Tinguely had both in her moldy basement apartment—both scales and mirrors—but she kept them packed away in Mayflower Moving corrugated cardboard boxes. Why unpack them? They were carefully ensconced in bubble wrap and to use them would only incite the kind of thoughts she could least afford at this point in her life.

****

Tinguely Querer forgot to pack her favorite pair of jeans.

It was not an accident. She was already gaining back the weight she had lost and she did not want to face the day when she would not be able to zip up those lovely teeny-tiny-hipped hip-huggers that made her slim derriere look plump against her thin waist and clearly visible ribs. The fact that skin hung loosely from her stomach and her face looked oddly lined and hard was not something Tinguely wished to confront right now.

When she saw herself in a bathroom mirror, she lightly crossed her eyes so they would not focus.

Her new "skinny" jeans had absolutely no history. She was not sentimentally attached to them.

Truth was, for the last three or four years, she had great difficulty in feeling attached to anything.

Jeans. History. Childhood. Her favorite pop tune: "Oh Very Young."

Cat Stevens converted. He left behind the empty searching, the jeans, the inability to look himself in the mirror—

No one could quite pin down what he had converted to. It was more about converting to something and leaving something destructive behind.

Tinguely left the cigarette lighter she had grabbed from the hot asphalt of the parking lot of Toot'n Totem while she spent time waiting in line to buy enough gas to make it home. People were expecting a dollar jump in the price of gas. Hurricane season.

Memories. Visual echoes. Tinguely could pack a suitcase with all the things she had left behind.

She could fill the cupboards and closets of a small house with the stories and cautionary tales she had heard, and then ignored.

****

Tinguely hated turning 30.

She turned 30 on the road, so she celebrated by ironing her favorite white cotton dress shirt using the hotel iron and ironing board. Instead of a birthday cake or even cupcakes, Tinguely bought a head of cauliflower and put it in the refrigerator.

She then decided to go on a long, long run. She would have hoped for endorphins to kick in, but no one really talked about "runner's highs" or "endorphins" any more. The idea sort of played itself out in the late 80s. Now all that was left was a veiled threat of what would happen to you if you did NOT go on a joint-crushing run, or a psychosis-inducing bout of chanting OM MANI PADME HUM.

30 was a bad age. She was too old to feel euphoria about the unknown, and too young to feel the smoothing effects of ennui and lower estrogen/progesterone production.

Her dermatologist recommended a deep peel.

****

Tinguely had left behind many things over the years.

Most of the time, she was not even aware that she had jettisoned them. She was even less aware of her compensatory behaviors. She did not see herself as she made dramatic, but probably impotent gestures, possibly in the same way that two buddies on a leaky sailboat bail water overboard while their boat sinks and sharks circle.

The waters of her past reflected the dull flat eye of the hammerhead shark. Her own face was lost to a trick of sunlight and deep pools of light bent but not thrown back into her own eyes.

One time, on a small, cold skiff, she almost vomited overboard. The waves were choppy, the adrenaline rush had long turned tiresome. She kept herself together that time, and left nothing behind except a certain type of innocence about the sea and its behaviors. Fishermen died in these parts, they told her later. She was not surprised. The fish on ice at the southwest Iceland coastal town of Grindavik had no smell.

What were some of the things she had left behind over the years? Here was a list:

- A swimsuit she bought at the Blue Lagoon just north of Keflavik, Iceland, that reminded of her of loneliness and hair that felt like silicified straw.
- A comb perfect for untangling hair damaged by chlorine or ultra-high concentrations of minerals put into solution when briny steam met the lava from a pull-apart zone.
- Singleton earrings, almost always part of a set that represented a deeply sweet, sentimental, full-of-promise set of interactions. The pair always seemed to break apart. Nothing new there, right?

Tinguely hated losing a single earring, and thus was stuck trying to make do with a half dozen or so mismatched, highly clashing singletons.

Beautiful in pairs.

Ugly on their own.

It was the moment in which tears should have come to Tinguely's eyes, but she felt her throat grow warm with a low, involuntary laugh.

"I have a lot of secrets," Tinguely said. She fell silent and looked at the floor.

The young man she had met at the exhibit hall smiled and joined in, "Hey, who doesn't?"

He didn't know what he was dealing with. Tinguely was Tinguely, and there was not any way to avoid the eventual splashy collapse. It's the nice alter ego/counter to falsely positivist views of reality. Yes. And, she started to remember just why she liked talking to small groups, and, yes, even large crowds. She felt strangely comfortable there—as though all of the facets of her personality finally had voice and had an eager, listening ear. Yes, you had to have at least twenty in the group to get that sort of satisfaction. Otherwise it was better to stay home alone, reclusive, interacting with those twenty or so voices/personalities via tweets and feeds on the Internet and her smartphone. Busy, busy chatter. That's what she was all about. It was not at all what she was about. If only someone would take her by the hand, reassure her, and say she was loved unconditionally—she did not have to continue having to "prove" her merit, or "earn" their love by how much she paid for it, in both cold hard cash and in time/tears/tendons.

When she was 16, her mother, alarmed by her daughter's self-destructive dieting and exercise, enrolled her in a weeklong intensive program called *Institute in Basic Youth Conflicts*. The gist of the program was along the lines of:

"God loves you. God accepts you. You are perfect in God's eyes, and you have gifts that are just waiting to be unwrapped. Once you open those packages, the gifts will start paying dividends.

"You've got to believe, though. You've got to believe in the gift of yourself. You are who you are because you are special and you have a special mission, a special destiny. God loves you. Sacrifices have been made. People have died for you—you are unconditionally and unequivocally accepted.

"So, start accepting yourself!! Don't stall around! Move, smile, dance, be free—express yourself! Share, give, listen, and above all give freely of the free gift of love that God gives to you. Love means acceptance. Love means tolerance. Love means smiling when you don't want to smile, but you know your neighbor needs a smile. Now. It's okay. You can cry all you want. Yes. Now. God is love. You are loved."

"But I have a lot of secrets," she said.

"Ha! Smile. That's why God loves you all the more. Your secrets are what make you special. What has made you ashamed is, in reality, the key to your success. So—well—I'll keep your secrets. And you can keep them, too. There is nothing to fear. There is nothing to be ashamed of. You're who you are because your special skill set is just what it takes."

"It was a miracle," her mother said. "I thought we were going to lose our daughter. She was very, very sick from her eating disorder. But something happened there, in the Institute—and she came back to us. The very next year she was a straight-A student, and she won scholarships to college."

More importantly, she started smiling. And, she made friends. For the first time in her life, people called her.

She was not utterly alone.

A Page from the Journal of TINGUELY QUERER

The Big Questions

How do we tell good from evil and right from wrong?

What is reality?

How do we know what we know?

Which professions are most ethical and which are the least ethical?

Why is being a circus clown a morally better choice than being an Olympic athlete?

It may have been her imagination, but Tinguely Querer noticed her hair seemed to be becoming finer, more flyaway. She also noticed that she was able to maintain muscle tone—to even look slightly ripped—while spending almost no time at all lifting weights. The most she did any more for her upper body was to close the door to her office when she was feeling groggy after lunch, and do ten sets of ten pushups against the edge of her cheap and grotesquely heavy veneer-over-particleboard office desk.

She always had the sense that her life was interchangeable with a Hal Hartley film. She lifted the book she had bought because it was cheaper than a ten-pound dumbbell, and it gave her nice definition in her deltoids.

As she watched her muscles flex in the mirror, she wondered if she could find the email addresses of the editors of the weighty tome she had in her hand—the *Norton Anthology of Theory and Criticism.* She would like to express her appreciation of their Catholic, all-inclusive view of the world. Her leg hair was definitely thinning these days. She could go weeks without mowing her legs and they looked just fine.

For fun, and to see if her muscles bulged, she did a yoga pose—*Anjaneyasana*, a forward lunge with arms in the air. Whenever she did yoga, it had a very oddly familiar feeling about it, perhaps because when she was in junior high school, the warm-ups and cool downs after dodge ball or some other humiliating "team" (read "gang up on the weird kid") sport, were meditative yoga poses and asanas. It was a good thing. It helped her ignore it when she was duped yet again by a too-friendly face asking her overly solicitous questions—which she answered in good faith until somewhere along the line she realized she was being mocked, not interviewed. She was their entertainment, their sport, their way to feel still in control and

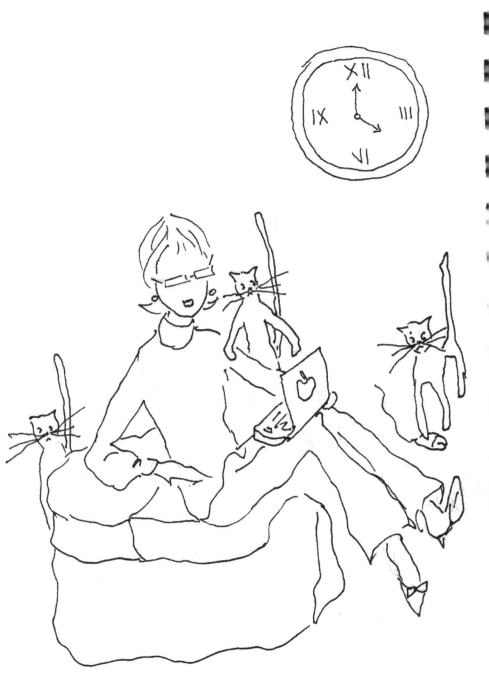

on top of the world. (sigh)

If her hair really was fining, and if it were due to some odd shift in her hormone production, should she feel awkward about the change? She liked the word "transmogrify"—it had the convenience of meaning to change shape, but it also had the sound "ogre" embodied in it, which is exactly how she felt these days. Perhaps she should live under a bridge. Menace billy goats who happened to clippety-clap over the bridge. The nice, ripped body would be nicer if she had someone to share it with. But, who had time?

Her favorite Hal Hartley film was *Henry Fool*—about two people—a garbage-collector poet and a hack writer, and the unexpected encomiums that result when work gets out, goes viral....

She used to care about having work go viral, but the only way she could get her YouTube videos to go viral was to do reaction videos from the highest-ranked videos of the day and put in all the same tags; and then not care when all the scathing insults streamed in from people who fell for the bait and switch. Her best viral video was a reaction video to the news of a Siberian tiger mauling a zoo patron.

Today there was Great White Shark attack in California. A surfer's entire leg was detached in a single, ghastly, scary movement of jaws and razor-sharp serrated teeth. How? Why? Let's look. A 20-foot-long shark can exert a bite force of over 18,000 newtons (4,000 LbF).

In Hal Hartley's sequel to *Henry Fool*, the garbage collector's wife, Fay Grim, finds herself in an odd situation. The camera angles reinforce the oddness—they incorporate "Dutch angles"—in common terms, the camera is all catty-wonky ... it's in the wrong direction. I guess the filmmakers had a reason for it, but the reason was perhaps a bit banal. Don't be afraid of your geography. She went to the Dollar Tree store to load up on five-dollar movie candies selling there for a buck a pop.

Instead, she bought a gallon of Crystal Geyser water. It was all in the interest of world peace. Be free. Accept yourself. Love everyone like a brother or a sister. Keep a disciplined approach to life and your goals/personal mission (if you have one).

There were one or two scenes not shot with Dutch Angles. By that time, she was tiring of catty wonky for catty wonky's sake.

The camera shot flat, straight-on shots, nothing "Dutched" with angles; nothing made dizzying with too much dolly work. She needed to tell someone she loved him. She dialed. No answer. She texted. No answer. Same with email. Nothing.

As she descended into a slough of despond, she realized that she could be her own friend, her own companion. Spend more time in the gym. The body that emerges can be your own special friend. Does that make sense? It shouldn't. And the fact that it does not is good. The most beautiful place on earth is thirty floors up overlooking the Caspian Sea and the Icheri Sheher—an old walled city and a drowned fortress, the Maiden Tower, said to have housed an Azerbaijani variant of Rapunzel.

Then she realized she was not able to "un-Dutch" herself. All angles, all perspectives were destined to be high-angle and to not conform to those of the world. Ah. Nice. Eventually, with 20/20 hindsight, this will look to have been prescient; somehow foretelling just what she needed to experience and to do in order to get to a place where love is love and that's all that matters.

Catty wonky.

The glove on the sidewalk just past the concrete drainage area had not moved since someone dropped it there a month ago.

Yes, it had been a month now. A long, yet brief month. The thumb of that cotton glove was the same color as a dried chrysanthemum leaf on the bush on the edge of Tinguely's patio. Yellow, maize, amber, gold. Petals like metal brushes on distressed silk.

The stars were out. Tinguely Querer sighed. It was going to be a long night. She half-hated being back. Her hometown did not quite feel like her hometown these days, and she was not sure why.

It was probably not worth probing, she decided. If she did, it would only lead to thoughts that reinforced the sense of helplessness that was gripping her lately.

The back patio and miniature courtyard were quieter than usual. Tinguely looked at the Sheridan replica chair she had purchased years ago after an unexpected windfall of cash. She was glad she had turned the cash into something she could still use, even years later. The quality of the chair could not be argued. The way it felt when she sat in it was more important to her than she may have felt comfortable admitting, even to herself. The smooth wood and the warm leather brought to mind idealists in smoke-filled rooms hashing out the details of the Declaration of Independence, and then, later, various drafts of articles of incorporation, of the Constitution.

Martha Washington.

It was an intrusive thought, but probably appropriate, thought Tinguely.

She liked to think of Martha Washington as the real architect of the Declaration of Independence and the real framer of the Constitution.

****

Quote from Thomas Paine: *A long habit of not thinking a thing wrong gives it a superficial appearance of being right.*

****

With a sinking feeling, Tinguely recalled the Hiroshima and Nagasaki memoirs she had read as a part of a project to help people reconnect themselves to their humanity and to bridge the artificial gaps people construct when they label themselves and huddle together in like-striped masses in a false sense that collective isolation somehow protects.

Reflection in the sliding glass door. Sleepy-sad, almost unrecognizable eyes glistened. It was very quiet. Upstairs, she had placed a small bed with a hard (euphemistically dubbed "firm") mattress in a room she used for storage. Scented oil emanated into the unadorned, monk-like room. The porous sticks of balsa uptook the scented oil and then diffused the aroma into the warm, still air.

"The pillow inverts its own flannel: chenille and carved velvet are standard fare in my interior," said the voice on the radio. "Smooth it down," the voice continued. "It is time to go to bed."

Tinguely looked up at the sky, then again at her reflection in the sliding glass door, wondering what the future might hold, but then, trying not to wonder. Yes. No. Wondering never got her anywhere.

Unimaginable change, with events so irrational and strange that only absurdism could come close to representing it. That was what Tinguely thought. She wanted to find something amusing in it all, a point of gallows humor, but she could not. It was impossible to neutralize the feeling of so much collective fear and outrage. She had never witnessed anything like it—not even in countries like Uzbekistan after independence, where professors sold their prized academic texts for the equivalent of a dime and a pensioner, sweeping a banya outside St. Petersburg, made the sign of the cross in great Orthodox gestures as Tinguely gave her the equivalent of twenty cents.

****

Trust only movement. Life happens at the level of events, not of words. Trust movement. (Adler)

****

"Movement doesn't protect. Life happens in random ways," thought Tinguely. The moon was full. Her heart was equally so. Yes, to the bursting point.

Two men at Starbucks were discussing their problem. A man kept showing up at Trinity Church. He was threatening them.

"The cops won't do anything. They say he's not doing anything illegal," said the guy.

"What is it he wants, precisely? What is he angry about?"

"He is dangerous. He threatens me. He calls my cell phone all the time. He wants something. He wants someone to listen."

"Listen to what?"

"No one can tell. When he speaks, I can't follow him," he said. "Let's get back to our Bible study, okay?"

"He doesn't like it that you were once his friend. Then, when you got religion, you dumped him. That is all."

Random thoughts, intrusive thoughts: Tinguely reflected

on how they ebbed and surged. Thoughts were often irrelevant, as were false explanations and, well, false consciousness. Tinguely was willing to assert that the only times that meant anything at all were the times when she was only movement. The movement could be anything: tears, breezes, sound waves emanating from laughter ... and a night like that night: a cool October breeze like a stiff bristle brush.

****

Quote from the American Revolutionary War by Thomas Paine: *If we do not hang together, we shall surely hang separately.*

****

Tinguely recorded herself on her BlackBerry: "Note to self on a night like tonight: my hands, belly sweating in spite of myself, inside myself, darkness—running, running, running."

Then she turned to T. S. Eliot's *The Wasteland* and shed a few tears, not for herself or her civilization, but for the ineffable beauty of the night, the stars, the sky—before interpretation, before over-determination of meaning(s).

It was beautiful, and still, Tinguely never felt very comfortable here.

Coco Chanel spritzed onto her wrist. The sky was not midnight blue, shot through with dreams, with motives made transparent by a softening of the feelings she constructed out of the peeling Polaroids she called her past. A bookshelf painted black with chinoiserie.

Tinguely looked up at the full moon. She inhaled. She exhaled.

Her phone rang. It was her father. They spoke a bit, and then he hung up.

****

"Dad, this is how it is. I run, run, I am running. I trust the movement, the pattern. I don't trust anything else. It is my life. I trust what I see. But now, all I see are Saturn, Chiron, and a constellation beyond detection, beyond comprehension."

Static followed the dial tone. No one. Absolutely no one there.

But then, the whisper came across her cell phone. It was something she did not know how to address, but knew it was important.

The voice: "The stars are out tonight, Tinguely.

"Oh, and Tinguely—the planets are there, too, only brighter."

The only obstetrician in the small Texas town admitted five women in five hours to the local hospital. Each had a different threat to her pregnancy. Will the hospital run out of beds? It's possible, someone said. We did not smile.

It is unusual to have so many obstetric emergencies at the same time. Is it a full moon? Sunspots?

My first thought was that it was from the smell scraped off the surfaces of the slaughterhouse north of town. Someone said they installed low-water systems for conservation, to go "green." Doesn't low water mean it's harder to hose off all the blood? I admit I've never seen the inside of a slaughterhouse/packing plant, so I have no idea how they use water. Do they have high-pressure hoses? I'm all for green.

The wind is blowing. I have to tell you it is not necessarily a good thing. However, I want to face the wind whenever I have to, and I want to look at it – even when it's cold and frustrating – as a blessing and a life-giving force. The wind turns the turbines on the south edge of town. Yes, I'm in northwest Texas, again, in the Panhandle nirvana of the essential elements: earth, wind, and the fiery sun....

Naoya Shiga: A Dark Night's Passing. The orphaned boy met his grandfather, who held his fate in his hand. The boy was six years old. To him, the old man looked thin and cruel. Taking an instant dislike to one's imposed patriarch does not strike me as wrong.

A Page from the Journal of TINGUELY QUERER

There was an interesting headline yesterday: Vultures and Yard Fish.

Did you know that there is no such thing as a "flock" of vultures? Groups of vultures are referred to as "committees."

After the hurricane, committees of vultures feasted on the "yard fish" washed up onto front lawns.

I told him about the condo two doors down. It was for sale. He bought it. It was like being complicit in my own stalking.

It reminds me of baboons.

Did you know it's not a "pack" of baboons, but a troop?

Troops of baboons tend to overpopulate the South African game preserves.

* * * * * *

I'm playing Russian roulette with the few worn-out eggs I've got left.

"It snowed and hailed at the same time. Six inches."

The urgency to write. Get the words out. Do it. Do it now.

Her words had vigor. They had muscle. They had nowhere go. So here she was, writing as though she had only five or six minutes to go before the end of the world. End of the word. Which was worse? It was a slip of the tongue.

And the sky turned to ash.

"It snowed and hailed at the same time. Six inches."

Just don't ask about the cattle. It's not very easy to think about the things we have to think about.

*****

A stunning woman with long gray-blonde hair pulled back in a fundamentalist chignon, long purple skirt gracing her ankles, lovely patent pumps: she came straight from a prayer and praise service. Healing. It was all in the body. But perhaps the room was in the mind. Yes. Perhaps. She stood near the front entrance, next to a Happy Meal poster and a troop of small baboons masquerading as a girl's softball team. It is all what we need to look at, how we need to think.

More lovely women in skirts, long hair, and prairie fervency. It is what we think it is, is it not? Yes, no, yes, no.

A small, pale smile. And then the long table they had inhabited cleared in an instant. They left the way they had come. In solid white SUVs and the kind of pickup truck that has room for passengers in the back.

Angels, of course. Angels riding in the back seat (and not in the bed of the pickup, nor on the roof). Angels have got to be practical these days.

****

It was the same asphalt track she had run on exactly a year ago. What was different? Not much. The same old farm equipment, the same antique tractors and gas separators. All the same, just a bit more rust and a bit less paint to boot.

The landscape of boom-bust was largely interior. Nothing showed on the surface. Not even the tears. Not even the blood from internal bleeding. How many men did she know had suddenly ruptured inside? The scientific term was something obscure. The medical term was aneurysm. The real word for it was love.

That's all you could feel at a time like this when people needed it so, but were not able to share their fears with anything or anyone.

The yellow lights over the convenience store illuminated the wildly fluctuating price of gasoline.

The things that never seemed to change were the hallucinations. The chaotic chips of kaleidoscopic funhouse neon were the closest thing to reality these days.

Bad dreams are what you can wake up from if you learn all the tricks of the trade.

"And what are those?" asked the woman at the counter. She was asking about the latest Snack Wrap flavor. Tinguely heard it as something else entirely.

Not that it mattered.

****

At first, she thought someone had strewn posies all along the asphalt track. They looked like clutches of flowerets, miniature bouquets. They were the kind you used to make for May Day

165

and tie to your neighbor's doorknob.

Then she realized they had made their way through the asphalt. The delicate green had made its way through the thick, hard, black petroleum byproduct.

There was a lesson in that. She did not know what that might be.

****

"You know where you are, don't you?" asked the retired professor who had made millions teaching petroleum geology to non-geologists around the world.

Tinguely shuddered. The air smelled of old heater treaters and an abandoned refinery.

"This is where I want to build my museum," he said.

"You need an attraction," she mumbled. "Something to draw the people."

"We will have a real, working miniature drill rig."

"You need a mummy or a cloned sheep." Tinguely thought of pickled two-headed pig fetuses and nine-legged frogs. That would never work.

"I want to honor the oil industry."

Tinguely looked at his face. It was innocent, fervent, plastic. She thought of an old Tarzan movie where Jane and another skimpily clad jungle lady were rescued from quicksand.

"La Brea Tar Pit," Tinguely smiled. "That will appeal to everyone. Let people experience what the mastodons experienced. The saber-toothed tigers. The Pleistocene cave goats."

"It was sort of a one-way street, wasn't it?" asked the mild-mannered professor, surprised.

"I set out glue traps for mice. It's the same concept."

"I think that if it is to be successful at all, we'll have to design a tar pit where people can experience it, but then leave alive. They can't be covered with tar, either. They will track up the nice clean floors," he said.

"I used to think dinosaurs were demons," said Tinguely.

"There were no dinosaurs in La Brea. They were sixty million years earlier. Just Pleistocene beasts from one of the many ice ages during that time," he said.

"I drove by La Brea. It's in Los Angeles. There's a Bob's Big Boy across the street. They've used the Big Boy as a set for a lot of Hollywood movies. Hollywood. The twentieth-century tar pit."

She said it, pretending to be hard and defiant. The image of the house mouse squirming in the glue trap haunted her. She had set the trap in her desk at work because she was tired of having her letterhead gnawed on and stained with rodent urine.

Tinguely could have been one of many stuck in the tar pit of Hollywood dreams or, alternatively, deliberately lured into waist-deep glue just because she happened to inconvenience someone by stepping all over their papers, their ideas.

Death by glue trap was not appealing. Death by the tar of one's own fantasies was even worse.

Asphalt was a different matter. Hard, it gave her a chance to run herself into oblivion, always staying on the surface.

****

The blood-red moon turned white as bleached linen.

The seas, hot red flames in the setting sun, turned as blue as alpine violets.

Tinguely rubbed her hands together. They were dry. Too much time had elapsed since the last time they had touched a living surface. A small, pale child peered out from around the corner.

Flowers defied the wind. Weeds burst through the asphalt. She was not going to give up. She would swim upward through this thick, dark, tarry night until her tendrils unfurled for the light of dawn.

"It snowed and hailed at the same time," the man repeated.

"It was such a blessing. We needed that precipitation," said his wife.

Just as Tinguely needed her precipitous awakening. Breathe. Hold tight. Don't breathe. Then breathe again.

It was all about love, after all.

The Wildcatters

On a generous day, you think of them as freethinkers. On a tight-fisted, grudging day, they're crackpots and a danger to themselves and others (mainly their heirs).

They're the wildcatters. They invest in high-risk, high-reward ventures. They look for elephants (giant oil fields), and they want to find giant oil fields and "resource plays." They're looking for legacy plays – an oil field, a rich gold deposit, a reservoir the size of Delaware.

They believe in their own technologies, which they themselves invent – crystals to dangle over a map, Reichian orgone accumulators, Chakra-energy-driven wands and devices.

Wildcatters are at their best after their 80th birthdays.

I've long learned I should not be fooled by their appearance – the wildcatters dress themselves in L.L. Bean, but sometimes old-school rancher, and sometimes Rotary Club. In a nutshell, they look conservative, straight-laced, Sunday school. But the straight-laced among them predeceased them by decades.

If you're tense and by-the-book, do you die young? Or does your behavior somehow reflect an inner malaise, a chemical imbalance, or spiritual malaise that puts you right in the crosshairs for a heart attack in your 40s or 50s or 60s? I don't know.

All I know is that I think they live longer because they give themselves permission to believe whatever they want to believe. Sure, it might look like "magic" to the outsider. It's not mainstream, and it opens a world where we can live with freedom from the facts. We don't have to be slaves of science, they seem to be saying. We ARE science. That's all there is to it.

Their belief is both exhilarating and frustrating to the children, nieces, nephews, grandchildren – if the children try to implement the same philosophy, they will soon find it to be ruinous. When you're starting out (and don't have your own successful business, cash flow, nest egg, retirement), it behooves you to play the game, learn the social norms and the societal paradigms, and play them as best suits your personality in the best way you can.

Apparently, you have to play within the system and learn how to find joy in the acquaintances you make, the milestones you can share with others, and the team-spirit energy that leads to building something tangible in our material, phenomenal world.

The wildcatters will have nothing of that. They want to transcend the material, phenomenal world. They want to have power, and they want all the things any good Faust would want – infinite knowledge (mainly of arcane things – think Witches' Kitchen), infinite power over the elements in our world, and the ability to cast spells (think Prospero), infinite treasure-hunting for precious metals, stones, substances, and infinite power to heal (think L.L. Bean-garbed shaman).

That's not so out of the ordinary, right? Well, you might be surprised to know how many L.L. Bean-garbed gentlemen in their 70s through 90s believe in crystal power, have detection/dowsing devices, and claim to be able to heal by laying on of hands and by beaming chakra energy from their own bellies to a person through their image (a photo, for example). What do you do when, upon entering their home, they offer to check your aura, and then, if you offer them food, they measure its frequency (by means of their own frequency) to see if it is good or bad. That seems nice and harmless. It's all a matter of degree, I guess. Are you

Rub - a - dub - dub,

a devout disciple of Christ or do you claim to be Christ himself? I think we see the entire spectrum, and it's nice to let people have their beliefs.

Here's what people say: Insane people are happy people. They have the power of their convictions. On the flip side, insane people are unhappy people. Insane people are like blindfolded drivers riding on lawnmowers of paranoia.

You just hope that the charming eccentric who wanders around with a tolerant, "let your freak flag fly" cheerful bonhomie does not turn into a cornered rat, sharp teeth bared. I guess the one way you can turn your smiling, easy-going great-uncle, who wears aluminum foil over his breast pocket and carries around a crystal on the end of a gold wire, into a cornered rat is to put him in a cage. Anyway. The charming eccentrics are everywhere.

The wildcatters have outsider beliefs.

> Some claim to time travel.
> Others commune with spirits.
> Others spend time looking for treasure and cures for cancer.

They're kind-hearted, sometimes hard of hearing, sometimes detached as though they're focused on something else. Sometimes they're grumpy. That probably can't be helped. They've taught themselves the art of hallucination. They've taught themselves the art of living. Just don't invest with them or pay attention to their career advice if you have a deep need for conventional socialization and dislike stepping out of your comfort zone.

Perhaps one of these days, I'll be a wildcatter.

My Midyear Resolutions
(for July 21)

1. BE TRUE TO MYSELF. PLAY MORE. BUY MORE TOYS. Translation: get involved in high-tech and very visionary educational/literary projects that challenge me on at least three or four levels.

2. ENJOY WHAT I EAT, AND EAT WHAT I ENJOY. Slow down, sit down, and don't wolf it down while standing up. I'm not a cow (yet).

3. RECORD VIDEOS OF DAILY LIFE. Share them. But don't try for the "big moments." Record five-second snippets of daily scenes encountered in my typical travels and rounds.

4. WRITE A CHILDREN'S BOOK. Do not center it around vampires, werewolves, zombies, luisons, or other undead, unless the publisher absolutely insists.

5. SET SAVINGS GOALS; REDUCE MY OVERHEAD. Achieve the savings goals. (In other words, set them low).

6. TRANSFORM THE WORKPLACE, MAKE THE WORLD A BETTER PLACE. Think of solutions to hamster-wheel jobs and hamster-family workplaces. Do what I can to help people prepare themselves for jobs that have a chance of resulting in something. Who wants to think that their only thrill in life is seeing how many sunflower seeds they can pack into their cheek pouches? It is important to take the high road. Don't become a hamster mommy or daddy who emerges from its shredded Kleenex nest with a hunk of newborn hamster baby tails hanging from your mouth. Be nice to your co-workers, even if it is difficult. It's all about overcrowding and overpopulation. Why

else would the hamster mommy or daddy eat its young - live spawn - the very night they're born? Sometimes the cage is too small, the cube farm is too cheek-to-jowl and invasive. Help people spread out.

7. WARN THE WORLD OF THE DANGER OF EXOTIC PETS. An African black mamba is not a good pet. Don't encourage genetic engineering and the development of such aberrations as glow-in-the-dark anacondas.

8. WATCH MORE FILM NOIR. Why? I'm not sure. Noir heroes are anti-heroes. People are flawed. No one gets out without bumping up against a secret.

9. SMILE, EVEN IF I DON'T FEEL LIKE SMILING. Assume a relaxed, passive position when my loved ones are speaking to me. They will think I'm listening and have acquired (finally, after all these years!) an ability to hear what they're saying – and – more importantly, accept it. I know in my heart of hearts that I have not (and cannot) acquire that ability. It's better to learn how to multitask mentally. I can mentally rerun what I'm choreographing for fun dance routine, or visualize tennis and the serve I'm trying to learn.

10. IMAGINE WILD HAIR, STRIPED PANTS, AND A BIG FLOPPY HAT. Develop a new character to draw as I illustrate the children's book I intend to write.

META-GOAL: Smile, chant, pray.

She lost her identity, so she had to steal it back.

It happened the same week the crystal skulls at the British Museum were sent to a lab for testing. Someone suspected the real ones had been stolen and replicas put in their place.

That did not help Tinguely Querer.

In the short-grass prairie in the high plains north of Amarillo, Texas, she forgot her wallet, her garage door opener, her last paycheck, and her mother's maiden name.

Tinguely was forced to steal back her own identity. In the process, she learned things about herself she never knew. It was a deeply unpleasant experience.

****

A girl has got to eat, right? Even if she does not officially exist....

The woman at the local Food Court was disorganized. Tinguely noted how dirty the place was. There were flies in the taco salad, chunks of salsa on the greasy stainless-steel countertop. Tinguely was offended by the entire scene and thought of calling the restaurant's headquarters. Every other Food Court she had ever visited was absolutely immaculate.

In contrast, every single Burger Prince she visited in this part of the Texas Panhandle was cramped, dirty, and awkward. Men and women used a single, unisex bathroom. Perhaps it was the norm. The toilets in government buildings in Tashkent, Uzbekistan came to Tinguely's mind. A porcelain chamber pot was positioned in the center of porous concrete, a water closet with a chain for realizing the water was positioned overhead. Toilet paper was not a consideration. The only positive thing was that the area for washing one's hands was expansive, with scalding hot water and three or four varieties of soap. Tinguely had no idea why she had that memory.

The tune of "A Horse With No Name" floated through Tinguely's head.

Losing her identity had unintended consequences. She started to forget. The years she had wasted in a loveless marriage began to slip away. No memory, no pain.

The years she had scrambled to create herself as a brand and to "build the brand" were gently erased, blurred, rubbed out.

****

A deeply tanned man with lean lines and a kind face drove past farmhouses and neatly painted barns. A round Shaker barn caught his eye, and it made him think of the woman he had committed his life, heart, and his "troth" to, just before something inexplicable happened.

He would never forget her. Someday he would find her.

****

After the action-adventure movie featuring a quest for an ancient Mayan crystal skull was released, it was determined without a doubt that the life-sized quartz crystal skulls the British Museum had acquired in 1890 were fakes.

According to legend, and the interpretation of glyphs carved on a light green jade-appearing onyx, the end of the world would occur in the Mayan calendar year of 2012, when all twelve crystal skulls would be placed in alignment with the stars.

No one asked if the jade glyphs might be fake, too.

Someone assumed that the original was a fake. But then it was clear that the original had been stolen and replaced by fakes.

****

Tinguely turned on the radio. It was a Sunday evening. Someone speaking in Spanish was explaining that God speaks in parables to mankind. The voice continued in Spanish: "God has knowledge of all things."

Tinguely looked down at her hands and had a sudden craving for a cigarette. Grabbing a pack from a light plum-colored leather pouch, she extracted one, lit it using the cigarette lighter in her car, and rolled down the window. The warm breeze carried the scent of sage and half-remembered rain.

The voice continued: "You have been given a glorious victory so that God may forgive you for your past."

The words made her uncomfortable. Reaching to change the channel and turn off the radio, Tinguely found, to her surprise, that the radio was not actually on at all.

Slowly inhaling and exhaling, the cigarette slowly burned to the end. Reflecting upon the drought conditions, she decided to extinguish the cigarette in the inch of old coffee in the McDonald's styrofoam cup in the mug holder conveniently located near her right hand. She did not want to inadvertently start a grass fire. The sound of the cigarette sizzling out made her think of the crinkle of impossibly thin paper.

****

Tinguely's boots were vaguely western, vaguely 60s bohemian

hippy. Cowboy, with hand-tooled designs, the boots had a few painted onto the beautifully tanned and buffed leather. Four-leaf clovers were positioned over each toe. She hoped they were making both a fashion and a political statement.

"Luck goes to the lucky," she said to the woman who brought her a few packets of ketchup.

She was in a truck stop off I-40. It was not easy to make her cash last, but she did not know who to call. By this time, all phone numbers, names, and even her own name had slipped away from her.

A slender man approached her. On his face was an expression of recognition and deep joy.

A dozen crystal marbles cascaded from a pocket deep within Tinguely's hobo pouch-styled leather bag. Someone in a call-in talk show was discussing how it did not really matter if the Mayan crystal skulls are originals or replicas—either could just as easily be used in bringing on of the end of the world.

As the tiny orbs scattered and bounced on the pavement, Tinguely noticed they were not cat's eyes, nor were they perfectly round. Instead, they were the oblate spheroid shape of skulls, or the earth.

A Note from Tinguely's Journal

"Logic is not a body of doctrine, but a mirror-image of the world. Logic is transcendental."

Ludwig Wittgenstein

"I need to predecease my grandmother."

It was an intrusive thought, completely unsolicited and unwanted. It was also illogical.

My grandmother had died when I was three years of age.

I was raised by my wildcatter father and a succession of housekeepers and private violin tutors, which is to say I raised myself, or, as I prefer to put it, by wolves, making me the "wolfling" – incapable of nurturing or mothering anything except like-minded wild things, of which I had met a total of three in my entire life, which now spans thirty years.

Logic is not serving me well these days.

The skies were overcast. The night before, the rain came with hail.

Today, the wind pushed gray into the corners of blue and chased the light bagatelles from the spring, replacing them with vestigial winter, the kind of archetypal chill that reminds one that life is not transitory at all.

We think of life as fleeting, but is it?

If anything, life is more permanent than the human mind can comprehend: life is passed on from mind to mind, in an endless chain of acquired consciousness. The natural, the authentic, were the stuff of fear and persistent sadness.

The cool skies opened up. The clouds hung low, their bedraggled edges scraping the tops of tall oaks, narrow evergreens, cottonwoods, and catalpa.

Bitter magic was in the air. Sweet water in the raindrops, dark venom in the nectars. She walked slowly across the garden, her footsteps echoing on the flagstones.

****

Tinguely closed the lid slowly. The jewel box had a velvet lining that cradled the simple gold chains, the platinum circlets.

Weather was changeable. Gold and platinum were immutable.

Her own qualities were something she was just beginning to discover. They were something between hopelessly refractory and utterly immutable. Joy was sometimes part of the equation. But, sometimes, it was not.

Joy was mutable.

Everything depended on him.

Draw, draw together, practitioners of mechanical arts. Call

them axiom-mongers, natural divinators, algebraical celebrants of the new earth. Take hold, grasp the new seepages of sorrow, of inverted birth. Draw upon what the Greeks called *techne* to imbue them with movement, with sparks, with light.

When he was in her life, a full spectrum of colors and possibilities burst into life. Together, they created the shimmer of oil and water. Rainbows appeared. A droplet smeared out on the surface of clear liquid comforted her with its multiplicity of hues and bands.

Together, they were strong. Francis Bacon would have classified them as "new compilers, seeking the causes or natural divinations," the "clear and easy discovery of the virtues and parts of bodies."

When he was not there, she longed for him. Each night, she slept with her books, with her warm pillows, comforted by narratives that surged mystery into her fingertips.

Do not fall out of the sky.

Be able to float in and fall—right on the runway. You learn from people. Fly high-lift ratio aircraft, with lots of forgiveness. Just fly. Just soar. Just realize where and how we are.

When he was out of her life, even for a matter of hours, she was aware of the fact that their rainbows, contained in a sheen of oil on water, suddenly collapsed back to black.

The love of her life took her hand. He kissed the fingertips, her wrists.

"Consider the former labors and collections…. Direct new experiments of a higher light, more penetrating into nature than the former. These we call lamps."

She recognized the quotes. She wanted to match his erudition with witty repartee. But something told her that to do so would be counterproductive.

"Can you go with me to the park? I want to see the azaleas, breathe in the scent of hot honeysuckle," she said.

He was aroused by her, but sometimes he still considered it

inadvisable to let it show.

"You're so lovely," he said, in spite of himself. He saw her—her face, her body. That was one thing. It was an entirely different thing to tell her what he really wanted to say, what he really saw.

What he saw was more intense. It was her essence. He could not even say what she really looked like. What he could describe, though, was her essence, and her effect on him.

****

The armadillo scurrying across the highway cheated death yet again. The armadillo was not built for speed; the little hard-shelled animal was a wobbly torpedo—careening mass and acceleration as it hurtled over the asphalt and other concrete surfaces of pure desperation.

"You are the love of my life," she said. Then she talked of crossing highways. Her voice was calculated to provoke him, make him feel simultaneously protective and judgmental.

He had mixed emotions. He loved the feeling of desire. He hated the feeling of helplessness.

Life was not as easy as Greek myths made it appear.

At the same time, Greek myth made life easier to understand than it really was.

The truth was, she loved him, felt compassion when he was conflicted, and when he was troubled by the contradictions in his own heart. Tinguely smoothed his turbulence.

"'Tis a pity I'm who I am," she said to him.

Her line of thought annoyed him, but he thought of her sweet body and forgave her.

Things were going the best possible way they could go, given the random multiplicity of their texts, their world.

"Let it go, my sweet," he said.

Vanished Without a Trace:
Clowser, Hurricane Hunter

Stats and Facts:

87 percent of missing aircraft go missing in the Bermuda Triangle.

Intense supercells develop between high- and low-pressure air masses.

In the transition zone, it is not uncommon to find "electrical fog"—static electricity so thick it looks like fog.

Some scientists have speculated that horizontal electrical tornadoes form tunnels of dark energy.

****

Tinguely Querer had decided to buy old Clowser's farm. She still remembered the night his barn burned down and the stories that flew like hot sparks searing images into the mind, burning the edges of memory.

Old Clowser was a recluse. Rumor had it that his family had homesteaded the 160-acre patch of South Canadian River bottomland. He owned it outright, being the only child of the original homesteaders' only child.

Old Clowser himself had an only child—a son, a pilot who disappeared in the Bermuda Triangle while flying his small instrument-laden jet into the eye of a Caribbean hurricane.

He was a "Hurricane Hunter" for NOAA, and he paid the ultimate price for poking the eye of the hurricane. No one even remembered the name of the hurricane that took him into some unknown dimension—probably shattered to bits, but the conspiracy theorists preferred the idea of alien spacecrafts sucking trespassers into "their" airspace.

Tinguely sensed that the unsolved mystery of Clowser's son's disappearance could be solved if only she could take possession of the farm and the new barn they built on the ashes of the old.

****

"Why cash? Why not a loan?" asked Evalina Baugrozen.

Evalina was an attorney, albeit not a very confident one. But something about Tinguely gave her newfound "brass" and spunk. She was not experienced enough to realize that Tinguely had made her a fantastic deal—not because of generosity, but because of sentimentality.

"I want to get this done. I want to close quickly," said Tinguely.

Tinguely had just advised her father not to sell his wheat farm in Grant County, Oklahoma, with a "take or pay" contract with a pipeline company to sell the gas produced from the Red Fork sand. The wells were in the middle of the Cherokita Trend.

"You've got a good deal, Dad. It is a rare occurrence when minerals go with the surface." It was something she said often to her father. In fact, she had used his wheat farm and oil production as a case study for one of her courses in her MBA program.

Evalina looked at Tinguely.

"What is it that you see in the old Clowser place?" asked Evalina.

"It's complicated," said Tinguely. It was not really complicated at all. She wanted Clowser's farm.

Tinguely's judgment was compromised by her sentimentality. She liked to idealize her childhood. Her early years were lonely. She learned to read music before she could read words. She

185

was four and reading music, playing the piano in recitals. Mrs. Crow, her teacher, considered Tinguely her prodigy. Things might have progressed, but Mrs. Crow's husband graduated from the University of Oklahoma, and he and his lovely wife moved to a town that had offered Reverend Crow a position in their parish. They accepted the position, even though Mrs. Crow abandoned a number of budding young musicians. Tinguely was just one of them.

The world lost something when she left behind her young charges.

Did she have any idea? Did her husband know? Of course not. Their psyches had been tainted by "righteousness"—they were just so convinced of their moral authority, that they had taken the "high road" even though there was not one scrap of evidence to support them.

Flash Memory. Return to the summer her parents moved to the house at the end of an isolated cul-de-sac, positioned like a strange apostrophe to a developer's fantasy, between wheat farms and a strange, overgrown set of fields, farm ponds, farm house, and big barn.

So, what happened to young Clowser, the Hurricane Hunter? Some scientists liked to conjecture that the Bermuda Triangle is a place where space warps back on itself. Dark energy becomes a force that pushes time and space, not just wind and rain and hail. Several scientists hypothesized that the atmospheric conditions resulted in tunnels of dark energy and a virtual space warp.

Some suggested that the plane was pulverized by the high winds, and young Clowser himself fell to earth (or water, as the case might be), like a twentieth-century Icarus, whose hubris was not his own, but was inherited—by brazen, transgressive folk who believed that just by casting their eye on a particular place or space, they could "own" it—regardless of previous or existing claims.

Clowser's son was an Amelia Earhardt without the glamour and publicity. He was a risk-taker. He went solo. He was an aviator for reasons other than the love of soaring on rivers of air. He loved punching into the place beyond the edge. Kick into another dimension. Smack life into your truest heart. What does that mean? Don't look. Don't care.

****

When Clowser's barn burned, someone said a fireball shot out of the barn door. It occurred because of hay dust.

"You know, hay dust is as flammable as gasoline," said one of the firefighters who was interviewed for *The Norman Transcript*. "It's the same thing that can happen in a grain silo. Static electricity can ignite it. It can happen at any time."

Tinguely read about St. Elmo's fire. It was static electricity that danced along the sails in old clipper ships and the galleons favored by buccaneers. Tinguely wondered if there might be more St. Elmo's fire in the Bermuda Triangle than in other places.

Was "electric fog" something you could find in windy places on land as well as sea? Could a tornado churning through the Texas Panhandle be accompanied by roiling electrical fog?

She had the feeling that there was some sort of energy triangle that came together right where Old Clowser's barn burned to the ground.

There had to be a connection between the barn, the fireball, the Bermuda Triangle, and Old Clowser's only son, that intrepid young "Hurricane Hunter" who vanished without a trace.

****

"Tinguely, you'll be happy to hear your offer was accepted," said Evalina.

"Thank you, Ms. Baugrozen," said Tinguely. She pronounced Baugrozen so it sounded like a large mastiff's bark.

"Now that you have the land, do you have any plans?" asked Evalina. "Do you plan to put in a housing addition?"

"I'm going to build a barn."

"Farming? That doesn't seem like you, if you don't mind my saying so," said Evalina. She snapped her black patent clutch shut after replacing her pen and her BlackBerry.

"Not farming. Hurricane hunting," said Evalina.

"Well, I think you may be barking up the wrong tree if you plan to build a barn to do that. Unless, of course, you fill it with computer linkups to weather satellites."

"I'm still working out the details," said Tinguely.

"Well, do what you like. The Clowsers were well-thought-of in their day. They homesteaded the place, you know," said Evalina.

"Yes."

It was done. The deal was inked. Now all that was left was to slip into a horizontal tube of dark energy and seek the place where space warps back on itself.

Then she could do it again. Watch that ball of fire, that fireball of inflammable hay dust, and determine if it happened the moment knowledge itself sparked—or perhaps self-awareness sparked, ignited, and caused the seekers of consciousness and perception to vanish without a trace.

Memory Is a Problem:
The Embedded Narratives in the Decade-Organized "Hits"

Jimi Hendrix. "Voodoo Child." Is it heresy to say that
this song does nothing for me? Sure, I understand the
greatness, the individual talent, the spiraling pass that
makes it all the way to the end zone of a bliss that has
appropriated and/or bowdlerized Romanticism all over it.

I'm only listening to the recording because I have no
choice. I'm in a gritty, Bohemian restaurant that has a raw
veggie wrap I like.

Long-term memory is not static. Even autobiographical
memory is dynamic, subject to change. I'm not sure if
that means that one's ability to recall is variable, or if the
memories themselves are variable.

I'm intrigued by the latter. The implications of a protean,
constantly morphing memory are fascinating.

Jimi Hendrix has now moved on to "Easy Rider." I can't
remember who did this song. I don't much care for it.

I'm at a table next to a window partially covered by a
poster advertising a New Year's celebration. Two men
have just walked by – one is pushing a shopping cart
with clothing and other possessions. They both have long
brown beards. No gray. Does that mean they're in their
twenties or thirties? For some reason, I always think of the
homeless as being old, but the truth is, they're generally
not.

I remember having contact with homeless in Oklahoma
City. The parking lot I used was next to a detox center, and

men would regularly ask for a dollar or sometimes odd amounts, like 15 cents. In New York City, the panhandlers were not homeless, nor were they in Baku or in St. Petersburg. Instead, they seemed a bit like carnies – very well-rehearsed and organized. One Sunday morning two years into the Iraq war, I came across a ragged young man who was leaning against a brick wall somewhere off Rittenhouse Square. For some reason, I felt compelled to give him a ten-dollar bill. I think I was influenced by my time in Azerbaijan – it was fairly normal for people to stop and give money to people who were on the street corners asking for help. I respect the generosity of the individuals who give out individual charity. There's something about the panhandlers here, though, that takes me aback. Perhaps it has something to do with the fact that some are given to saying aggressive things and demanding a cigarette.

Can I trust any of those memories?

I believe I can. But, one has to say that it could be that emotional connections to the memory could mediate it.

Some sort of 70s anthem is blaring across the speakers. It is equally repellant. Why do I dislike "Classic Rock"? Does it have anything to do with associated memories?

Most people would say so. They would claim that the popularity of "greatest hits" compilations has to do with the fact that they trigger memories of pleasant times, of one's formative years. Music is like perfume, in their eyes. It triggers deep memories that you can't expunge, even if you want to. So, what you do is find the music that has the most pleasant cluster of associative memories and then you replay, replay, replay.

Good idea?

If memories are pliable and/or shape-shifting, doesn't it follow that every time you hear a song in a new context, the experience of listening to the song is mediated?

Furthermore, does it not follow that the emotional impact would also change?

Concrete example: If I first listened to Jimi Hendrix's "Voodoo Child" as a child in conjunction with confusing, rather menacing images and energies, would that always be with me? Would my experience change if I started to associate the song with exciting times in the summer – sitting outside eating dinner with friends, drinking coffee at a bohemian java bar?

Another song, some sort of ditty that is a clear borrowing from an Irish folk tune: "Mr Blue Sky ... welcome to the human race." I can't remember who wrote or performed it. Let's see. Think. Oh, yes. ELO (Electric Light Orchestra). It makes me think of other artists and the provenance of their inspiration.

Elton John admitted to having raided the Methodist hymnal for chord progressions and even melodies.

Memory turns into a self-delusion machine if we're not careful.

If we have associated memories – what are they associated with? The updated melody? The original? The variations that came later?

Rolling Stones: "Honky Tonk Woman." My memories associated with this song are of my older cousin from Vermont who came to spend a summer with us in Oklahoma. In my view, her presence was quite unwelcome. She occupied my bedroom. Her main goal was to go back bronzed and glamorous. This was before tanning beds – and – before she had experienced anything but a Northern sun. The Oklahoma August sun did quick work of her, and when I think of her, I think of her listening to the Rolling Stones, then baking in the backyard on my mom's favorite chaise longue. Later, she burned to a crisp, or at least a blistering ball of pain. Second-degree burns. I felt nothing but SCHADENFREUDE at the time (I was six years old). Later,

I got mine. Not realizing why the beaches of the Yucatan peninsula were empty at noon in March during spring break, I, a sixteen-year-old who should have known better, got so sunburned the tops of my toes peeled.

Memory is fallible. That's been demonstrated over and over again. It is remarkably easy to induce false memories as well. Why do I think I'm immune to it?

Perhaps "greatest hits" and perfume are reassuring simply because we rely on them as memory markers. They trigger memories – authentic ones, we suppose – and we rely on them to access a kind of "write-protected" part of our brains.

But, apparently, nothing is "write-protected" and your memories can be altered through the power of suggestion, without having to rely on any sort of physiological issue. So, there is nothing to say that my memories of my cousin and her taste for the Rolling Stones and the popular television shows of the day that featured teenagers in go-go boots and "mod" Herman's Hermits and the like have not been effaced or attenuated by my emotional need for a certain narrative to be associated with those days or times.

This seems fairly straightforward.

What is not so straightforward is how I'm supposed to move forward in a world where everything is fluid, where everything reinvents itself, and not necessarily in a way that benefits me.

The other day, I was listening to a program on the radio – the name of show was something like "Radio Lab" (see how I distrust my memory for my invented schema and the labels and shorthand retrieval, but I trust it implicitly for the narrative). It was the story of a woman who dated a man with face-recognition disorder. Coincidentally, the week before, there was a story about a professor who had face-recognition disorder. They could neither remember nor recognize faces. They would have intense difficulty in life because everyone was, in essence, a stranger to them. I suppose the pattern recognition part of their brains were sadly compromised.

I had a few questions for them. Could they read maps? Could they recognize where they were on a map? If face-recognition disorder was anything like the problems I had in field camp trying to see in 3D with stereo pairs – well, I can understand the frustration. When it came to verbal recognition/description of lithologies, I was completely on top of it. To me, geology was a language and a discourse of explanation. My brain is comfortable with that. My brain is not comfortable with making my vision go 3D and/or contorting spatial relationships in order to make some sort of visual pattern. My brain is all about process analysis and language. I'm not saying that I can't recognize visual patterns, it's just that I think the maps we were supposed to use back in the 80s required too much visual extrapolation. For me, it was like using a slide rule rather than a calculator or, better yet, an abacus.

I'm acting as though the most important aspect of memory is autobiographical memory, and I have to say that I'm uncomfortable with that thought.

Perhaps the most interesting aspect of memory for me has to do with working memory – the place where short-term and long-term memory come in contact. How much of working memory is impacted by the limbic system – raw, unmediated urge – fight, flight, fornicate, feed. And how much of working memory is affected by desire?

I have a feeling that desire plays a very disturbing role in the function of the brain, particularly when it comes to the retrieval of long-term memories and the way that connections are made between prior knowledge, experience, and schema. I have a feeling that desire can reroute memories and make false priorities - which is to say that it makes certain memories rise to the top, while leaving others to hover along the bottom together with the other catfish.

I also suspect that if one does not learn to discipline one's own desire, one is fated to be stuck in fantasy mode – and eventually, one's memories will only be accessible through one well-trodden and very boring working-memory road – and one will end up remembering only those things that make one feel good.

Hmmm – does that sound like anyone you know?

I have a friend who has a favorite refrain: "Everything was better in the 40s." He was born in 1939, so I really question what sorts of authentic memories he has. He claims to have a very in-depth recall of the economic downturn of 1958 (or one of those years). I do not doubt him; what I see is a convergence of belief, desire, and emotional conflict (a recognized state of innocence mixed with an anger at the loss of innocence). So, in the end, what is emitted, with clocklike precision, is a rant about how wonderful and innocent those times were, yet how disappointing and hard – but the narrative that emerges from that uncomfortable juxtaposition is one that he invariably blends with a narrative of the Pilgrim's first winter, how honorable, pure, and heroic they were, and how ultimately sacrificial memory/consciousness itself is.

And, well, he never says it straight out in that way, but I will.

Memory and consciousness are sacrificial.

* * * * * * * * * * * * * * * *

So, here I am – writing this, surrounded again by music, but I'm in a different location – one that is warm in the way that an Art Deco boutique hotel can be warm. I feel transported back to a time when you can feel comforted by the solid clink of gold in your pocket and oil under your feet.

The music is different. Karen Carpenter is singing "Merry Christmas, Darling" in a way that brings tears to one's eyes – it is intimate and sentimental – what her contemporaries would have called "square" and, well, being the "square" person that I am (emotional and idealistic in a way that seeks approval from authority figures, rather than rejecting the approval of authority figures), I'm moved. I immediately think of my mother, and I'm sad that I can't call and talk to her.

Perhaps I will, even though she's not in a place where she can easily answer.
How many people dial up and talk to their dear, departed mothers?

Ah, yes. I'm starting to go down that road of memory mediated by desire.

I'm not sure I'm brave enough right now for that journey. So, I'll stay on the surface and remind myself how much I dislike the "Classic Rock" stations and the way people cluster songs around certain time markers.

Steppingstones

We look at our lives. We think we're at the beginning
or at the ending of something, but in reality we're not.
We're simply on steppingstones in the middle of a rushing
stream.

The rocks are smooth, and they are slippery. We can't
maintain our balance and stay on them, even though
we'd like to. After all, it's scary to jump from one rock to
another. The water is cold, and it is turbulent. The water
level rises and falls, making it also a matter of exigency
that we leap – preferably before we've had too much time
to overanalyze the situation and lose our initial, intuitive
understanding.

Oh, but it's not easy. As much as I celebrate the successful
leap and landing on a new rock, I am sometimes weary of
the constant readjustment, realignment, reassessment.

The water is rising again. It is time for action again. I
look (but only briefly) at the rocks behind me. It's not
good to look back because there's a certain introduced
disequilibrium in the physical act of looking back – not to
mention the fact that the mind starts to play tricks on me,
and I lose my sense of linear time.

The rock I'm on is pointed and it hurts my left foot. Three
stones ago, I perched for quite awhile on a long, smooth
stone. I now appreciate it, but at the time, I felt the
steppingstone I was on was too big – I was too exposed – I
felt vulnerable. The waters started to rise, and I leapt.

Then I leapt again, again, and again. So, here I am now. The
air smells fresh today. It's a bit foggy, and I hear the hum

of cicadas and a strange bullfrog twanging – it sounds like large rubber bands being snapped.

This is not the best place to be, but I've made it work — for as long as I've been here. The sun is coming out. The fog is burning off. Ah yes, and there's a mini-rainbow in the mist.

Bufanda

"I don't believe you!!!!"

A shrimpish young woman with a gravelly voice was growling into her smartphone, and the raspiness of it startled Tinguely Querer out of the dreamlike thought-drift she was having about silk, warm skin, and Cajun-spiced rice with golden raisins.

They were fogged in at Houston's Hobby airport. Fog in Dallas was delaying all the flights, and the last thing Tinguely wanted to hear was that someone was making a connection—be it physical, temporal, emotional, or logistical. Being stuck at an airport was a painfully disconnected experience.

Tinguely had dozed off while reading something about British literary giants in the 1930s, and the fact that many had a penchant for "disinterested" contact. Disinterested contact was code for consensual flagellation.

What about non-consensual flagellation? The concept sounded dismally familiar. It sounded like life-in-the-world and a post-consumer culture. We can advertise anything.

We buy what claims to protect us from eternity.

The air smelled of "Buffalo Hot Wings"—the bar and grill's logo had a cartoon buffalo with angel wings on its hump. Feel the burn. Then fly.

****

Tinguely was making a recording on her computer. She was going to upload it, then send a link to the message, which would, like all good messages, be equivocal and subject to interpretation (and projection).

Leviticus Martin was far away. He was most likely asleep. It was the worst time of year, and he had conferences to arrange, cases to settle. Tomorrow was a specially big day. For that occasion, he planned to look especially disheveled. It was his way of taking the edge off; taking the point of the knife away from his perfectionistic streak.

Tinguely and Leviticus had become friends, despite Tinguely's dad's misgivings.

Leviticus was a master negotiator in matters of estate planning. The people in his meeting would be busy dealing with the cognitive dissonance his appearance engendered and would not be able to focus on the work at hand. What kind of attorney fails to dress for success? He often wore the same clothes he wore to the gym. That's when he performed his most stunning magic.

Leviticus had a penchant for extra large distressed t-shirts and baggy wind pants that often got caught in the edge of a sock, stained yellow-brown by coffee with half a dozen Mini Moo's creamers stirred in.

Tinguely had a penchant for Niki de St. Phalle art and perfume, and she liked to run in long-sleeved shirts, even on the hottest, steamiest July—but that was another story.

Tinguely was on her way to Barcelona.

****

Tinguely and the Leviticus Martin were probably meant for each other. But, their perverse rabbity natures kept them bounding off in absurd directions. So, Leviticus was in the hot, sultry fog of a Michigan summer, and she was dragging herself down the jetway onto a flight she had impulsively booked using frequent flyer miles and courage borrowed from an account of early modernism in Spain.

Even high on a hill overlooking the Mediterranean, the Barcelona air smelled of diesel and bitter orange. Tinguely had traveled here to see Parc Guell, the place the architect Gaudi had decorated with his own unique art nouveau vision. The walkways were filled with broken ceramic shaped into fantastic mosaic lizards, toads, and asymmetric shapes approximating tables, chairs, benches.

It felt odd to be alone. Out of balance. Vaguely disoriented. A heart with a surface like antique glass. What was the word that would describe the surface? Crazed. Or, more realistically, shattered.

****

The Picasso Museum had replicas of Picasso's *Guernica*, and stories of the bombs the Fascists dropped on a village, and the carnage, the female body parts, the exploded horse shrieking in horror and pain.

Before seeing the work, Tinguely had chalked up Picasso's representations of women to misogyny and the fact that he had big, ugly trout lips that no one could possible tolerate. She imagined his mouth moving like a big, sloppy striped bass or a channel catfish when he tried to express his love.

Valor. Love. Bombs. A gutted bull. Blood in the sand. A gored matador. Love, longing, death.

Tinguely walked down the street. A thin woman wearing a dark-blue skirt, long sweater, approached Tinguely.

Her heart cracked a bit when she saw the woman. Her floppy skirt, the draping sweater reminded her, oddly, of her attorney friend, who was probably curled up in bed, his thin, muscular arms wrapped around a hypoallergenic goose down pillow.

"Scarf? Bufanda?" Tinguely realized the thin woman was selling scarves. She expected to see rather frayed, cheaply-dyed polyester. Instead, what she saw was the wild, rare fabric of

Scheherazade, Silk Road cargoes, and the magic that allowed Don Quixote to see a fair maiden and mighty steed when all around him were the tatters of sonnets Petrarch composed to his beloved Laura and a chivalric code gutted by cynicism and one big expedient betrayal.

"Yes."

The scarf was identical to the ones Tinguely passed over in the gift shop. There, they had cost thirty-five euros. Here, the woman said she'd sell one for five euros. Tinguely bought three. Each was a replica of Picasso's *Guernica*, but in different colors: orange and brown; green and aqua; purple and blue.

When she held them to the light, they shimmered and the clear, blue sky took on clouds in the shape of hearts and flowers.

The scarves were undergoing a metamorphosis.

"The scarves are changing shape–images. What is happening?" asked Tinguely.

"Son bufandas de la gran ventana. Ventanas al alma." They're scarves to the great window–window of the soul.

But the woman's Catalan was not something Tinguely could understand.

****

"It was a completely pointless trip. Next time, remind me I'm being foolish when I say I want to spend a weekend in a faraway place," said Tinguely as she draped the blue and purple scarf over her shoulders.

How was it that skin was softer than the silk of the scarf? She was not sure if it was a good idea to bring up the subject. Instead, she kissed him softly.

The smooth brown utilitarian flooring he had put in reflected the light. Leviticus Martin put a hand on her leg.

"Didn't you enjoy Barcelona at all? You love art and architecture."

She looked down. There was a small twig at her feet. It was not really a twig, but a part of the root system. The appearance was deceptive. It had a direct route to the root system of the entire tree.

Tinguely held up one of the scarves to the light where a full moon illuminated his small courtyard.

"When you look through the sheer part of this scarf, what do you see?" she asked him.

Leviticus looked at her oddly.

"Do you really want me to play this game?" He paused, held up the scarf. "You may not like what I see."

He looked. Then looked away. Looked again, this time at Tinguely.

"You were holding a bouquet of white roses. But it's not real. We have no roses. But when I look—well, there they are again. White roses."

"Look at me now. My face. What do you see?" she asked.

"I see your face. You have a strange tattoo. A black rose."

"The one you were thinking about getting on your left hip?"

"Yes. I now see why it would have been a mistake."

"What do you see now?"

Leviticus paused.

Magic. If you held the scarf in a certain way, as you looked through it, you could see images from your past, present, and possibly even the future.

****

The floor was slippery. A woman wearing a sky-blue cotton shirt, sleeves rolled up, was dipping the mop in a pail of soapy water.

Didn't anyone bother to explain that suds and surfactants were deadly on a slick granite floor?

Tinguely felt herself slip. As she caught her balance, she thought of riding a bicycle through ice and oil-slick patches on a dark, moonlit road.

A Note from
Tinguely's Journal

It was the day after Thanksgiving. Dad and I went to the cemetery south of Noble off Highway 77 where the Querers are buried. I didn't want to go empty-handed, so I suggested bringing silk flowers. My dad had already donated all my silk lilies to the church, so that was not successful. We ended up going into the backyard to his favorite rose bushes and cutting off three yellow roses and one red rose. We put them in a vase, which we brought with us.

The goal was to try to decide on a headstone. What dimensions? What color? What kind of design?

As we stood at my relatives' graves, a woman drove up with a clutch of red and white silk poinsettias. She took out the yellow and orange chrysanthemums and replaced them with the red and white blooms.

"It's funny. Since my husband died, I don't decorate for Thanksgiving or Christmas. He was all about it. But, well, I don't know."

She placed the Thanksgiving chrysanthemums on the ground. "If they still look good, I like to share them with little Roger over there," she said. "He never has anything on his grave."

To tell the truth it was the first time since my grandmother passed away that I had brought anything out. It did seem very sad to see her grave – no marker, except for the little temporary marker with a photo taken years before. The dirt was compacted with mud cracks and a couple of thick tire tracks. I blocked the intrusive thoughts that started to push their way in.

"It's tough," I said. "It brings back too many memories."

I invariably thought of my grandmother during Halloween, Thanksgiving, and Christmas. My grandmother made a few things for Thanksgiving that seemed to be fairly unique – fruit-and-nut salad and, if I remember correctly, pistachio jello. Lemon meringue pie was also a "must," with the most amazingly fluffy meringue.
Cooking is chemistry.

The day was not warm, nor was it inordinately chilly. The cemetery had a remarkably warm, soothing feeling, due in part to the fact that it was bordered on three sides by pastures and a couple of herds of tranquil looking Black Angus.

At least 60 percent of the headstones had flowers or other decorations. There were a few flags, and one seemed to have an assortment of toys.

I was surprised to see how many names I recognized – one was the assistant branch manager for the bank I have used for the last twenty years. Her husband was buried just three rows up from my mother. Her name was next to that of her husband, along with the dates of their marriage. He passed away in 2005 – I remember her telling me about it, and how tragic his last few weeks were, with complications from chemotherapy. Five years ago.

Can she ever remarry? Does it seem odd that she would be buried next to her previous husband? I guess not – I mean, I know they had at least a daughter together, and at least one grandchild.

I'll definitely bring something for my grandmother's grave sometime before Christmas.

In Kansas

Some things are up to us (eph-hemin) and some things are not up to us. Our opinions are up to us, and our impulses, desires, aversions—in short, whatever is our own doing. Our bodies are not up to us, nor are our possessions, our reputations, or our public offices, or, that is, whatever is not our own doing.

Handbook of Epectetus

Tinguely knew she had a strange job, but she never expected it to take her to the places she was visiting in her quest to lease mineral, water, and wind rights.

Last night, it was tacky biker bar outside Wichita, Kansas, that had dirt-brown floors and smoky mirrors that reminded her of Schenectady, New York.

Today, it was in a Subway sandwich shop adjoining a Kansas medical clinic that was fortress-like rather than frumpishly genteel as one might expect on the outskirts of a sagging suburb.

"Just sign here," said Tinguely. The woman she was talking to made her feel uneasy. This was not usually the case. Ordinarily, she would pause for a moment and ruminate. Not today. There was something in the air that made her want to get out. It was not the trademark Subway smell of baking bread, pickled peppers and meatballs. Instead, it was something that turned the air murky, made her eyes water as though in contact with dilute pepper spray.

"I don't want a check," said the woman. She was wearing a red Nike sweatshirt and navy wind pants with parallel green racing stripes.

"You don't want to get paid?" asked Tinguely. "We have to give you consideration; otherwise I'm afraid the lease agreement would not be binding."

"Cash," she said. The woman fingered the rings on her fingers and glanced at her watch.

"Okay." Tinguely hesitated. She was not comfortable with this. It was around twelve thousand dollars. "Cashier's check?"

The smell of meatballs began to overpower the smell of baking bread. The early afternoon sun shining through the plate glass window was unpleasant. Sound of the radio. Sound of a woman shouting.

Tinguely glanced at the clinic. The parking lot was filling up, not with cars, but picketers holding signs with grisly photos of aborted fetuses.

The woman across the table seemed oblivious to what was going on outside. She opened a small notebook, took out a felt pen, and started to take notes. Under her notebook was a slim paperback: EPICTETUS. The sunlight refracted as it passed through her dangling Austrian crystal earrings.

"I had no idea," said Tinguely. "Guess the guy doesn't have to advertise. They do it for him."

No response from the woman. Brown and blonde streaked bangs hung over her forehead, grazing the top of her glasses. Her brow furrowed.

"I've always considered such doctors to be freedom fighters," Tinguely said. "Unless society takes it too far—as in the case of China. One child per family. Strictly enforced."

The woman scribbled in her book. She looked up.

"No cashier's check. Cash." She wrote something in large letters: EUDAIMON—the "happy" life.

"Paypal? Credit card?" asked Tinguely.

"No. Cash. It's a great deal, and you know it. You're getting the wind, water, and mineral rights all at once. You and your dad are real operators. I'm doing this because I have to. And, frankly, I want to," she said.

"You don't even know my father," said Tinguely.

"Oh, you would be surprised. I have known him—known of him—for a long time. He's got quite the reputation, you know."

Tinguely felt shudder run up her spine. She wasn't sure if it was irritation or shame.

The woman continued, "Yes. Your father claimed to be healing someone I know by putting her photo in an old 35mm film canister and aiming healing energy to her. Crystals, clay, some sort of ionized water. I don't know. Don't want to know. She was taking radiation treatments. Cancer. Not sure where. In the liver, maybe pancreas."

Tinguely stared at her. "What happened to her? Did she die?"

"No. Did radiation anyway. Plus cyberknife." The woman fingered her earrings. Her moisturized skin looked flushed. "She thought she'd hedge her bets though. She let him beam her energy. She also wore crystals and a necklace of very strange herbs."

****

The skinless hand reached up toward her neck. It started to squeeze. Tinguely felt her tongue swell.

The contractions continued. They were hard. They were premature. Foreboding nothing by terror and misery, she dreaded the moment of actual childbirth.

When it happened, she was suffused by nausea; not the normal nausea that accompanies extreme pain, but the nausea that accompanies extreme grief.

With one flesh-ripping contraction, the bag of wet tissue forced its way out. She felt something's tongue on her ear. She heard the thick, foul promises, the torpid wad of dreams.

She looked down. Half-expecting a birth cry, Tinguely

was not at all expecting what she saw. The sac fell open. Dry dust, ash, and the char from burned hair woofed up, making a miniature mushroom cloud of unspeakable stench.

A dry pouch like gray parchment.

A cloud of ash. Of the sort of smell you don't want to smell. Ever.

And then Tinguely heard something she would never forget for as long as she might live. It was the bone clatter—the clatter of dry bones falling to the floor as her body expelled what it could in the childbirth process. Marimbas. Steel drums. Soft castanets.

The skeleton was terribly deformed, but one could still see what it was.

The most horrible thing, besides the deformity, was the fact that the fetus was completely dry. The sac itself was wet, but inside was a landscape as dry as the inside of a mechanically inflated balloon.

And then, Tinguely hemorrhaged blood and a clear fluid that looked like glycerin, but smelled vaguely like mint.

****

Shouts from the parking lot. Screaming. The sound of glass breaking.

"Is my car safe out there?" asked Tinguely.

"You parked out there? No. It's not safe. What were you thinking?" asked the woman.

"I had no idea...," said Tinguely. "But, even if I had, I still would have parked there. Gesture of solidarity. Looks like the clinic does late-term abortions. I think that is courageous."

"A lot of people think it's murder," said the woman. Her face softened.

"Sure. And a lot of people think that the mother's life

is worth nothing. She's nothing but a vessel for someone's sperm. They want to own procreative rights. No matter what. They don't care if a woman dies in childbirth giving birth to a headless, deformed creature, and in doing so, orphans her existing children."

"Ha. No one dies in childbirth any more. Medical technology has advanced," said the woman. "Your argument does not fit the prevailing facts of today's society or circumstances."

"I am against capital punishment. I am against 'eye for an eye.' I am against vigilantism," said Tinguely. "I also find myself taking a position—either moral high ground or moral low ground—when I don't even feel qualified to say one thing or another. Right? Wrong? I don't know."

"Don't you think adoption is a good choice?" asked the woman.

"Sell the baby? Oh. Yes. Absolutely," responded Tinguely. "Yes. I've seen that in action. In Baku, Azerbaijan, for example. There, women have surgery to 'revirginize' themselves. If they don't, they run the risk of an honor killing—if they're from the countryside."

"Multiple abortions. With each, the chance of obstetric laceration goes up. You see a scarred cervix. A mangled flap of tissue. A tear. You know what it means."

"I don't know what it means at all," said Tinguely. "This entire conversation makes me feel a though I'm going down a path that will take me to some sort of demented hothouse. Tiger-striped orchids."

"Terrible rape by instrumentation. Rough insertion of the sharp metal tube used to suction out tissue. Dilation and curettage. The woman twitched while in the stirrups. Just couldn't keep calm. Couldn't remain motionless. Lacerations. Lucky they did not perforate the uterus," said the woman. "Some don't make it. No one really knows, though."

"What does that have to do with anything?" asked Tinguely.

"Is there any way we can change the subject?"

"Some women bear their scars on the inside," she said.

The sound of rocks on plexiglass startled her. Tinguely looked down at the lease agreement.

"Do you want to go ahead and sign this?" Tinguely asked.

"Want to? No. Not really," she said. "Desire is something I feel terrible about."

"Let's go to the bank. I'll get the cash. I'll have to sign a form though," said Tinguely. "Dad will not like this."

"You do whatever it takes to get what you want, don't you?" she remarked mildly. She stood up. Tinguely noticed that her Nike Turbo running shoes were color-coordinated with her outfit, and she wore a hair clip in the shape of a Scottie dog, like former President Bush's black Scottie, Barney.

Security guards were moving themselves into position. They were a well-oiled machine, probably from so much practice, thought Tinguely.

She sighed. It would take two or three days to recover from this very unpleasant encounter. Even as she reflected on the reality of things, Tinguely could not put her finger on what made her so angry, nor could she understand why she flip-flopped on the core issues.

Anger was useless.

Tinguely took the signed lease, filed it at the courthouse, and then did her best to forget about the woman she had met in Kansas at the Subway sandwich shop next to the late-term abortion clinic.

Hobo

It was an unbelievably windy day in the Texas Panhandle.

The wind was from the south, which struck Tinguely as propitious for the wind turbine farm south of town, but not so lucky for the man on crutches carrying a plastic bag of either trash or his possessions, or both. His leathery skin made determining his age quite difficult.

Tinguely suspected he was homeless, but she could not tell. He had been sitting near the entrance of the store next to the Dairy Queen. The wind buffeted his ballooning trash bag and threatened to topple him.

During the Great Depression, the same man would have been called a hobo, perhaps a vagabond. He represented freedom, but Tinguely wondered if the people who chose a life unchained by jobs or steady income knew their very presence made people fear freedom.

They feared the kind of "freedom" that allows one all the mobility they can afford, but that also reduces people to a dense, poreless substance, like rock or metal, that sinks forthwith—straight to the bottom—when tossed into an ocean of water or people. It sinks without even leaving a splash, ripple or a spray of droplets.

****

"Will you go with me to Quartz Mountain?" Tinguely left a message on the phone. He was not home. She hoped he would call her as soon as he got the message. She wanted to spend the weekend alone with him, hiking the trails, watching sunsets, holding hands—the things she once thought were a greeting card type of love, but which now seemed oddly authentic.

Once she scoffed at grocery store greeting cards, calling

them trite, sentimental—a commercialized absolution of familial guilt.

But one day, while purchasing gift bags at Dollar Tree, the greeting card aisle caught her attention. Either greeting cards had changed, or she had—they seemed different to her.

Perhaps the difference was in the price point. In the past, Tinguely had always tended to purchase five-dollar designer cards—replicas of famous paintings, or ones with wry, tongue-in-cheek or campy humor.

What the dollar cards lacked in sophistication and paper quality, they made up for in naked sincerity.

The Dollar Tree cards were not cool. They were not particularly aesthetically sophisticated.

But, for some reason, they made tears come to Tinguely's eyes.

****

She needed it. She needed love (although she refused to admit it). Without it, she could easily become that dark, dense chunk of magnetite or dark granite-like dacite that would cut the water, uninterruptedly, straight to the deep, lightless bottom.

Without it, she was dense, never buoyant, never able to keep from falling from the nearest emotional ledge or cliff.

Without it, she was a vagabond of spirit. Her daily life was filled with the sparkly clatter of work, and those who did not know her may have confused her with the plugged-in electronic holiday decoration she appeared to be.

It had taken a long time, but finally she came to realize that the nice, busy machine she was (or had become) needed a heart.

Her heart was running the risk of going hobo. The possibility frightened her. She had to do something. The machine that was her body, her being, needed a heart.

It was far beyond a mind-body duality. Her mind had not become lost in search of transcendent things, nor did it seek higher ground.

Her heart had simply become lost, helpless.

She told him she did not want to be dominated. In reality, she was afraid of wanting something and losing it.

The idea of love gave her the courage to breathe.

****

The greeting card was printed on inexpensive paper, and the art was basic.

> Before I met you, each year was the same:
> > Spring, Summer, Fall, Winter.
> Summers were indistinguishable.
> Each Spring had the same daffodils.
> Fall flared and when the embers cooled,
> > I called it Winter.

> Since we met, every day, hour, minute,
> > second—has its own special hue.
> A rainbow, a kaleidoscope, a prism—
> > every special color is you.

****

The man on crutches made his way slowly back to the Dairy Queen. His plastic bag was gone. He held a large styrofoam cup in his hand, the lid appearing to leak, the straw cracked.

Within an hour or two, he would disappear from sight. His

If it's true love, a special price
for you, my sweet

essence would sink like a rock into the ocean of machines, animals, and people flowing down the highway. But perhaps it would not.

A dusty and very faded Volkswagen Rabbit pulled up, the driver beckoned to him. The man on crutches with the twisted leg limped to the open passenger side door and slowly got inside.

The driver smiled and gave the man on crutches a box wrapped with a bow, then handed him an envelope the size that holds greeting cards.

During the Great Depression, he would not be a hobo or a vagrant. He was someone's brother or son.

During the great migration—or transmigration—of souls in what we know as consciousness, or existence—Tinguely would not be a rock or a piece of metal.

She was one wing of a butterfly or a dove.

Someone should be the other wing. Together, they would comprise the heart.

****

He called her. He said the card she sent him touched him in a very unexpected way.

They set a date for Quartz Mountain.

Tinguely Querer happened to find herself in the clutch of Gamblers Anonymous leaflet distributors as she made her way across the parking lot of the Thunder Pony Casino & Resort to the tag agency where she needed to renew the license tag on her energy-guzzling-despite-being-hybrid SUV.

A voice louder than the others startled her.

"You gave us smallpox-infected blankets. So—" Long pause. "We give you casinos."

Loud booming male voice. Female voices, shouting.

"Uh, I'm not with them," she said, looking at the grassroots activists. They seemed sincere, but impractical. Their protest was doomed, thought Tinguely. She was not about to share her thoughts.

The security guard who intercepted the Gamblers Anonymous flyer-givers was approximately 6'2". He had blonde hair, blue eyes.

"So. Blondie! What tribe are you in?"

He said a name Tinguely had never heard before.

"Ha! They sell tribal memberships. How much did you pay for it?" shouted a woman with beehive hair, glasses, and tattoos on her arms. She looked like a tall, plump Amy Winehouse.

"Fakes. Frauds. Forgeries. Who believes in papers and pedigrees anyway," mumbled Tinguely. The crowd was suddenly quiet. Perhaps they had heard her. Tinguely felt her heart skip a beat.

*****

Inside the tag agency, Tinguely handed her check to a woman wearing a name badge, "Hi! I'm Johnita Dawn. Thank you!"

Tinguely sighed before going back outside.

"To tell the truth, I'm afraid of them," said Tinguely.

"You probably should be. Nothing's more dangerous than make-believe macho," said Johnita Dawn.

"You've got a point. Honor. Pride. Defending the Fatherland," said Tinguely.

"Yeah, especially when these groups are fighting over money," said Johnita Dawn. "It might as well be two gangs."

"Where are the real Indians? Where are the real gambling addicts?" asked Tinguely.

"They're not in the parking lot. I can tell you that for sure. If anything, these guys are just mercenaries. They've been put up to it." Johnita Dawn moved her arm, and the light caught the shiny silver of her bracelets. She was wearing a squash blossom necklace with matching earrings. A leather-tooled barrette held Johnita Dawn's silver-streaked light brown hair.

"Are you one of the tribal members?" asked Tinguely.

"Ha! By rights I should be. But I'm not going to fight for it. My grandmother was born on a reservation, but they moved to town, and her husband would not let her sign up. Said he'd lose his job if his boss found out he was married to an Indian."

"Wow. That's horrible," said Tinguely.

"Personally, I think it was smart. Her sister signed up. When her husband left her, and she went down to find out where she could get a doctor because she was about to have a baby, she was put in a hospital."

"That sounds okay—" said Tinguely.

"It was a mental hospital. They took her kids. All six. Adopted them to white couples who had enough money to pull it off. Then she was given a hysterectomy," said Johnita Dawn.

"I always thought those stories were exaggerated," said Tinguely.

"Nope," said Johnita Dawn. They stood in silence for a few seconds.

Sharp thud, scream, man shouting. Popping noises like fireworks or an assault weapon.

"Oh no. It's a shooting," said Tinguely.

"Don't worry. They do this about once a week. Firecrackers," she said. She inhaled loudly, then exhaled disgustedly. "Stink bomb."

"I didn't think that Gamblers Anonymous guys would be so aggressive," said Tinguely.

"Now you see that they're tipping their hand. They're not really GA. They are fronts for the new casino down the road—the River Pony."

"You'd think someone would call the police."

"Won't do any good. Sovereign nation," said Johnita Dawn.

"Oh. Right."

****

Smell of gunpowder. Fourth of July backyard fireworks smell.

The newscaster announced that the Creek Nation's oldest living member had just died at age 110. She was born in 1900. Pretty amazing.

Question: How often are the "hypergenarians" not the person they claim to be? How often is it a much younger person who has assumed their identity?

I am always skeptical when I hear the 105-year-olds discuss their lives – especially the ones who claim that the secret to their longevity is hard living – drinking, smoking, gambling, eating pork fat, donuts, deep-fried American cheese. They could get the requisite skinniness through bouts of anorexia and bulimia. Why not consider at 75-year-old imposter? Even a fifty-something pretending to be an eighty-something?

I'm sure it's been attempted, especially if there are entitlement payments in the mix (pension, headrights, oil and gas revenue, etc.)

Where there's money, there's mischief afoot.

* *

If I were compelled to pretend to be a 110-year-old, what would I do?

First of all, I wouldn't do it. I would not pretend to be an 80-year-old either. Not worth it. I don't want to have the conversations I'd be expected to have – boring historical ramblings and an invented personal landscape. The alternative would be to feign dementia or Alzheimer's. That would be a fragile defense against being exposed as an imposter. It would make me too vulnerable. Before I know it, I'd wake up to find myself in danger of having my own identity snatched from me, and an imposter installed in my stead.

No thanks.

* *

It's only tangentially related, but the idea of a person pretending to be a superannuated citizen who has, in fact, passed away in order to get her Social Security check, pension, and any other dividends or royalties that might be coming her way seems to have incalculable psychic consequences to the person who decides to shove their own identity and reality off to the side in favor of a secure income stream.

What ever happened to "to thine own self be true?"

I suppose whoever is willing to rebirth themselves is somehow dissatisfied with their personal reality.

Don't they realize it means they will never see their existing friends, family, and colleagues?

I guess it's considered the sweet end of the deal, if their life is really so bad that they must go down that path.

Perhaps they're old enough that they've lost everyone anyway and the person they're impersonating was their only remaining relative – a mother, etc.

Who knows? Seems lonely, and not as regenerative, or as materially secure as it might look to the person who is idly contemplating it.

The Starbucks, where Tinguely had decided to get a Venti decaf americano with four packets of Splenda and a solid splash of half-and-half, was in a boutique-crammed shopping center adjoining the city's most exclusive hospital, a compact high-rise complex of wings and new additions dedicated to specialties unique to a chunk of territory encompassing northeast Oklahoma, southwest Missouri, southeast Kansas, and northwest Arkansas. It was not a quiet place. Medevac helicopters landed regularly on the roof. The persistent chunk-chop-chop-chunk of blades cut large, anxious swathes of air.

It was New Year's Eve, and Tinguely was trying to finish a report her dad was waiting on. Her small laptop was perched in front of her.

She was having a hard time concentrating. She asked herself questions she really would prefer not to. Did blood drip from the door of the helicopter? Who paid for the medevac flight when the insurance would not? Why did all BlackBerry text messages have the same tone, causing everyone to look to their BlackBerry at each "booiiingoing"?

Tinguely took out a lime-green leather-bound notebook out of her peach-toned leather tote bag and made a few notes on the smooth cream paper. Writing in her lizard-green notebook was an extended metaphor for the quest to think oneself capable of responding to wisdom.

The idea that wisdom might exist at all in the here and now gave her pause. Could it? She preferred the blissed-out state of non-wisdom, non-thought. The image of lights encircling and imparting energy and joy. That was easier. It just was.

But she had to write. The dull ache in her heart was pushing her to do that.

I'm here—in the intersection of the fight for life and for

Does the individual matter? At times, Tinguely sincerely doubted it. Her own individuality was problematic. She knew her role in life was to serve. Was it to serve her son? Her aging parents? The people she might meet who needed a cheerleader? They needed lifting up, or they needed the kind of structured interaction that caused them to think, to analyze, to create things that lived in the world. It was about making something you could perceive, right?

Now, the paradox came in when she knew she had to serve, but the individual she had to serve was inevitably an individual.

Either way, Tinguely envisioned herself as a shiny, colorful hot air balloon. She did not think of herself in the role of a medevac helicopter. Why not? In a word, because she couldn't.

In her life, she lifted up people who were already healthy. They saw the rainbow silks, the heaving balloony body panting to lift off the surface of the earth, and they smelled the fresh air, felt the cool air stir the hairs on their arms, and they simply could not get on board fast enough.

The balloon really did not take them anywhere, and it did not actually give them a view of the earth they did not already know. They felt, however, heightened senses of themselves. They loved looking out from the basket, listening to the "whoosh" of hot air, and listening to yard dogs bark frantically as they passed over neighborhood homes.

Later, Tinguely's balloon riders bounded across the grass to the parking lot, eager to share their experience. Tinguely loved seeing the satisfaction on their faces, their renewed sense of self, the restored sense of beauty and order in the world.

Yup, that's what I can do, thought Tinguely. That's what my "job" is—at least in a purely existential sense, she thought.

Instead of feeling satisfaction, Tinguely felt tired. Who cared about lifting her up? Who would lift Tinguely up?

Inevitably, it was Tiinguely who watched the colorful silk collapse to the grass and then slowly scooped up the soft parachute silk.

Who fired the flames that would heat the air inside her heart and set her soaring?

No one. Everyone.

The question was almost not worth answering. Tinguely did not actually own hot air balloons. This was purely metaphorical. But the role certainly fit Tinguely's public self.

Her private self was a different story altogether. She was no cheerleader, or pilot of a glorious hot air balloon. If anything, she had a small cave hidden away in a snaky, thorny arroyo, where she lit candles at night and prayed alone as she watched the stars and the moon move across the sky. She was alone in her cave. In fact, Tinguely pushed away anyone who tried to share her tight quarters. She accused them of being invasive, controlling, pushy. Or she rationed the pleasure of their company in order to not want it too much. She did not want to crave what she could not have.

The cave was metaphorical as well. In reality, Tinguely was working for her dad. She was trying to focus on the report, but the medevac helicopters distracted her. The sound made her tremble.

And here it was again. A helicopter hovered overhead. The sound was almost deafening. Tears rose in Tinguely's eyes, and she turned to the corner so she could discreetly cross herself, even though she was not Catholic. Somewhere overhead, someone was fighting for something they couldn't have; and they were craving what could never be.

They wanted to be happy, healthy, autonomous, desired/ desirable, and, well, alive—forever. The energy of the world compelled them to long for and crave what they could not have. Why? Continuance and continuity were the frightening obligations consciousness pushed down into humans—as a race—as a clutch of dreamy-eyed tribe makers.

She expressed her thoughts to her dad. It was a quick call on her BlackBerry. It was not as reassuring as she had hoped. "Don't worry, Tinguely. You're only 30. When you're 45 or 55 and still have these thoughts and these patterns, you should start worrying. Right now—well—nothing to worry about. You just haven't met Mr. Right."

"Thanks, Dad. Yes. You're probably right," she said.

"Yes. Just keep your eyes on the prize."

"And what's that?" asked Tinguely.

"It's a supergiant oil field," he said. "You'll be rich. I have found one. The new methods are working. Just get the leases, line up the drilling contract, and we'll get started," said her dad.

"The price of oil is still in freefall though. The price has declined 70 percent."

"Think long run," said her Dad.

"Oh."

Another helicopter. Tinguely had to hang up. The noise was too loud. She thought about leaving and going back to where she was staying. There was a time when traveling would have pulled her out of her mood. That time was long in the past though.

She was not Muslim, but she appreciated Ramadan. Perhaps her problem was that she had not gone through the purifying self-control of Ramadan—the prayer, the self-abnegation, the fasting, the refusal to feast on food, bad thoughts, bad intentions—for 28 days.

Boingooing.

Someone's BlackBerry was bleating. She glanced down at hers, even though she had turned it off. She glanced at the floor. A wooden stir stick, a crumpled napkin, and a price tag from the American Outfitter store next door clung to the space between the tile and the wall. X-Large. $34.50. A tiny Ziploc bag containing a white pearl button. Clearly a shirt. A dress shirt. For a man? For a woman? A man was talking loudly into his cell phone. Tinguely thought about leaving before another helicopter flew overhead.

Boinnggoiing. Bleet!

Another BlackBerry from another table across the way. The messengers were all the same. The BlackBerry boinngoinngs were identical. The messages, though, would be different.

Repeating the thought, Tinguely scribbled into her notebook:

> *The messenger is always the same. The message is always different. Even if the words are the same, the message is unique. Why? The context, the sender, the recipient, and the medium are all unique.*

Tinguely told her dad she often preferred the messenger (the BlackBerry, the emissary) to the actual communication.

"The messenger is service-oriented," she explained in her journal.

Would anyone ever read her words? She doubted it. She had lost track of how many journals she had left behind at exotic roast coffee bars and Whole Foods salad-by-the-pound shops.

Perhaps she'd go and drive by the river, listen to AM Talk Radio. Here was a paradox. One might argue that the message was always the same, but in this case, it was not. In fact, the context and the receiver were always different. Sure, she was the same person, but the rant of the host would be mediated by the glorious glow of lights, the longing to share, and the bitter realization that she could not really share her thoughts with anyone. First, they may not be available. Second, they might twist her openness and desire to talk to play to their own agenda.

It was not that everyone had to have her best interests at heart, nor did they have to be in the service of her whims. However, in a world of equilibrium and balance, human invention and whole-heartedness, well, perhaps there might be a sweetness, a warmth of give and take.

These thoughts stung. The feelings they elicited were needle-sharp, sad. Tinguely looked up at the hospital, toward the helipad. She envied the doctors and the nurses. Their activities were so engrossing. They probably did not have time to entertain painful thoughts. Furthermore, the adrenaline surges would keep them in a zone....

> *What is it like to have an all-absorbing job—like, say, being a medevac nurse or helicopter pilot? Their job was to lift people up. They lifted them to, they hoped, a very dramatic change—snatching them from the bowels of certain death. It must be quite a rush to be lifted up by one's job as one lifts others up. When you leave the cocoon of your job (the helicopter, the emergency room, the emergency situation), how does the "real world" feel? Is it flat? Is it dreadfully open and empty? Does it leave you with a flatness, a lack of affect? Is it what occurs when all the adrenaline, endorphin, and other stimulating chemicals your body manufacturers have been used up?*

It was New Year's Eve, and Tinguely renewed her attempts to motivate herself and finish the report her dad was waiting on.

It had been a sad, empty day. Now the day was almost over. Twilight crouched around the corner, helicopter blades made their chunky chopping sounds as they cut through the twentieth-floor air to the helipad.

It was good to be alive, but conditions had been far from ideal for most people.

Tinguely realized, with a rather cottony thud, that everyone she knew would say "good riddance" to the year. The year had not been bad for her, just filled with rather unexpected and sometimes unwanted changes.

Booingoïng. Someone's BlackBerry went off. It was Tinguely's this time. She did not answer.

It had gotten to the point she did not like surprises. And, well, her BlackBerry was no helicopter. It was no soft, billowing hot air balloon. It would not lift her up. Or, well, more likely, it probably would not lift her up. Quite the contrary. It could crash her to earth. Catapult her into her cave. Better not to answer.

"You should always keep $20,000 buried in the ground," said Dad. "I do. If you don't, I'll lend it to you."

Tinguely was putting the lid on a metal case. They hit a bump in the road. She bounced in her seat.

"You see, we've de-industrialized this country to the point that we can't possibly hope to reemploy people. Recovery is not possible."

Tinguely had accompanied her dad to the field. It was a bright, crisp fall day. They were on the 160-acre quarter-section east of town that Dad had bought when he thought a twenty-million barrel field lay 8,500 feet below the surface. He expected low-gravity oil in the high-porosity, high-permeability Second Wilcox sand.

Persimmons were bright orange against the robin-egg sky. The air was crisp.

"Dad. A coyote."

A slender, brown canine loped across the field ahead of them.

"Looks like he's got something in his mouth," said Dad. He slowed the white Suburban and looked more closely.

"A rabbit. Or perhaps a squirrel."

He slowed the Suburban and they got out.

"We're going to see chaos in this country when people realize. Or perhaps we won't. There are plans to deal with all the people. But one thing for sure—the banks will not be open. That's why you need to have cash," he continued.

"How much?" asked Tinguely.

"Enough," he said.

Another canine ran through the field. This time it was a remarkably well-groomed Corgi. It, too, held something dead in its mouth.

"They're running off to bury what they can't eat right now," remarked Tinguely.

"Animals are smart," said Dad.

The breeze was sharp. The sky shone through bare pecan trees and made the red sumac leaves somewhere between neon and queenly. Thanksgiving was just around the corner.

****

Tinguely helped herself to an onion ring. She was not hungry. She did not like deep-fried food items. It was a way to deflect the attention of her lunch companions. If she made flowery, showy gestures as she ate the food, perhaps they would think of her as a boor and not pressure her to do things she did not want to do.

On the other hand, if they thought she was a boor, a climber, a person somehow pushed up into a reach of society for which she was not suited—either by birth, or by the university she attended—they would consider her to be easy game. She would be dazzled by pedigree. If she were capable of understanding pedigree, that is.

She was.

The two women were explaining their dream to build a museum. One had started a 501(c)(3) as a tax dodge, but was, at heart, too tight-fisted to make grants. Her desire to hoard everything was a problem. It extended to cats and beyond. She did not yet realize her five-year honeymoon was close to coming to an end. She was too busy fighting the city hall about her cats.

Tinguely realized it in an instant.

Build it and they will come? Hadn't that been done before? Where? When? In some latitudes, corn grew so fast you did not really even need stop-action film to see the stalks poke their way through the dirt, unfurl their leaves, press their way to the sun.

"Any mayonnaise for the onion rings?" Tinguely asked. The women looked revolted. One had just recovered from an infection caused by a liposuction procedure gone bad.

"I want to build the museum in memory of my dear Harvey," she said. Tinguely softened. She touched her necklace—a gold chain with a bar spelling the Sanskrit word for "Bliss." Most people would assume it was some sort of Kabbalah-esque amulet with words spelled in Hebrew. They would not think of Tibetan Buddhism or of devotion to Tara, the female Boddhisattva.

Would Tara approve of deception, of dissembling?

Tinguely thought of the gorgeous green light of Tara, the protective stance, the healing, soothing irradiant green.

It was far, far from a knotted red string signifying adherence to the Kabbalah or Jewish mysticism.

She liked Tara because devotion meant liberation—liberation for all sentient beings.

Ironically, Tinguely's motives were all wrong. She hoped to trap the women in the tight, close warrens of their own minds. She wanted them to trip over their own prejudices—favorable or not—and retreat.

Solitude.

Schadenfreude—even if at her own expense.

Tinguely layered mayonnaise, ketchup, mustard, and a fine layer of pepper on the thick wedge of onion ring. She bit into it, felt the grease spurt into her mouth, the vile pore- and artery-clogging fats deceive her with a temporary high of satiety and savory taste.

If someone were to kiss her now, they would notice a thin film of grease from a deep-fat fryer coating her lips, and even her chin and the fine, blonde hairs of her Northern European heritage moustache.

It would be the first step in falling in love. With her. With "not" her—the reversals of expectations, the surface belied by depth, perversity, underground waters, abandon.

Go forth and sin no more.

****

Tinguely's sister was out of parrot food. Usually, she had nuts, raisins, and dried cranberries to meet the needs of LouLou, Tinguely's large green, gold, and blue parrot. Unfortunately, her sister was out. Someone had eaten them, thinking they were snacks for anyone.

Parked at the street was a radio station mobile studio. A famous personality was taping a special program outside near the park.

"Hello! Hello! Hello!" croaked LouLou. She loved Tinguely. Tinguely loved her back. She ruffled her feathers noisily and squawked.

"Are you hungry?" Tinguely asked. She knew LouLou was out of food and had brought her raisins and almonds.

The parrot was eating Kashi mix, CornNuts. Then, to Tinguely's horror, LouLou started to eat the styrofoam packing peanuts that had blown in through the door as the wind blew it open. The radio personality's mobile studio seemed to be full of the stuff.

A noise. The mobile radio station.

Another noise. The parrot.

To Tinguely's horror, LouLou was gagging. She had choked on the styrofoam packing peanut and could not breathe.

Tears streamed down Tinguely's face. She did not know what to do.

****

Across the restaurant, a retired professor answered his iPhone, then excused himself.

"They're interviewing me about the new launch of the space shuttle," he said.

His unexpected absence gave her the perfect chance to trot out her pet idea to the other retired professor. It was an idea for another museum.

"You need something to pull in the crowds. A mummy. A cloned sheep," she said.

It was hard to imagine people wanting to come to see the Wild Mary Sudik, the Oklahoma City oil field discovery well that ushered in a boom in central Oklahoma as well as a miasmic dark haze for three days and three nights. The very air was flammable. Tinguely wondered what that did to people's lungs.

"You should have a living exhibit—a La Brea Tar Pit for the kids."

The professor snorted. "Wouldn't that get messy?"

"That's the whole point!"

"Real tar?"

"Absolutely." She paused. "The kids can dive for saber-toothed tigers and wooly mammoths."

He smiled. "I think you're going to have to use the kinds of balls they use in McDonald's kiddie lands. Tennis ball-sized plastic balls. That will keep the kids safe. They can dig for plush toys."

Tinguely pretended to like the idea.

"The price of admission will have to include a toy though," he said. "No one who finds a toy will want to give it back."

Tinguely thought about it. True.

Truth was, without real tar and real death, La Brea Tar Pit lost its charm.

At least, for her.

Elevator to Nowhere

The will to mastery becomes all the more urgent the more technology threatens to slip from human control.

Heidegger, *Die Technik und die Kehre*
(1954)

It had been a long day. Tinguely Querer was ready to leave her office. But the elevators were malfunctioning again.

Not relying on the technology to repair the new, streamlined elevator, Tinguely decided to take the old reliable workhorse, the freight elevator.

How appropriate, thought Tinguely, as she felt she was getting a bit husky these days. It was hard to keep up the level of exercise she needed in order to maintain her weight. She was nursing a strained foot from the "turbo Air" footwear that failed to live up to its promise of an effortless, injury-free run.

The lobby of the high-rise office building smelled of the latest "green" biocide used to keep the mold and rodent problem in check.

The freight elevator door opened slowly. Tinguely saw two men tumble into the door from the street entrance.

"You need to give me back my wallet. Now. I am serious." A sixty-something man was shouting to a young black man wearing a dark brown shirt and tight khaki jeans.

"You need to have a little respect. Respect. Now." The young black man was on the verge of hyperventilation.

Lalica, the evening receptionist, leapt to her feet. Lalica had dark brown hair, and she tended to wear floral blouses.

"Boys! Stop it right now! There is glass in here! You could get hurt!"

The young black man sank slowly to the floor, put his head on his knees. He was sobbing. The older man pulled the young man's shirt. "Give me back my wallet. You had no right."

The sobbing was disconcerting. Tinguely was uncertain what she should do.

"You had no right," sobbed the young man. The sixty-something man was frantic to get his wallet. He tugged on the young man's shirt, his pants, groped in his pockets.

"Don't take that—that's my new iPod!" wailed the young black man. "It's the only thing I've got that works!"

The malfunctioning elevator door yawned open wide to the dark cavernous shaft.

Pulling something from the young man's pocket, the sixty-something man darted toward the elevator, not realizing what the door had opened to. He plunged through the open elevator doors.

Tinguely dug out her BlackBerry. "911."

Lalica nodded. The young man continued sobbing, oblivious. As Tinguely dialed, the foot injured by inadequate running-shoe technology throbbed. The malfunctioning elevator door went into spasms of opening and closing.

"It's going to be hard to get through that," commented Tinguely.

"The fall probably broke his iPod," said Lalica.

****

Technology comes to presence in the realm where revealing and unconcealment take place, where aletheaia, *truth, happens.*

Heidegger, *Die Technik und die Kehre* (1954)

INFORM...

SURVEILLANCE
SOCIETY

Tinguely walked slowly toward the wall of mailboxes in the high-rise apartment building where she was renting a bedraggled two-bedroom apartment. A tenant holding a paisley backpack was fumbling for her key. A tall, slender seventy-something man held his restless Pomeranian.

"Bella. Relax. We'll take a walk soon."

Tinguely read the notice on the wall: "Water Off from 6:30 a.m. to Noon. We apologize for the inconvenience. West chase only."

"No water again?" Her voice was indignant.

It was better not to say anything. After all, there was nothing to add. Her words would not influence the functioning of the plumbing.

"Another suicide. They have to turn off the water. Some kind of repair," said the paisley-backpack girl tenant.

"Well. Having the water off again will surely inspire another suicide. I do not know why it takes them so long to flush out the drains." The seventy-something man was huffy.

"That's the third suicide this month," said Tinguely.

"The curling iron in the bathtub may have been an accident." The man did not seem to like the conversation.

"As was the death of the guy whose GPS unit instructed him to jump off the balcony from the 23rd floor?" asked the paisley-backpack girl.

"Our machines are turning against us," said Tinguely.

"Machines still save time," said the man. "I love my high-speed coffee grinder and my new microwave."

"Save time for what?" replied the paisley-backpack girl, darkly. "Degradation and mind games?"

The Pomeranian barked, whined, shook her head, and rattled her collar.

"Bella, is your ear still bothering you?"

The man's brown eyes watered, and he patted the dog's head lovingly.

"We just implanted a chip in Bella's ear. This way I always know where she is. She can't run away from me. Ever again."

"I wouldn't trust it. The tracking device," said the paisley-backpack girl, glumly. "Bella is a girl dog. Bella, tear that chip out of your ear! It will only oppress and enslave you!"

"My dear, your comments are most unwelcome. Bella wants me to be able to find her," said the man. He pursed his lips.

"I can't agree more. You've got to know your machines. You have to show them who's boss," said Tinguely.

Bella leapt from the arms of her owner. Her reddish-gold fur shimmered. She barked fiercely at Tinguely.

"Don't worry, Bella. I'm on your side. I know someone who wants to chip me." Tinguely looked down at her new Google phone which had built-in GPS, synched to Google maps. People in her Facebook network could tell where she was at all times.

She sighed. It was time to pay someone to take her Google phone and to drive aimlessly to random places, just to teach anyone who would track her movements that she was not going down without a fight.

It was not right to reduce her to a pixel on a digital map and make faulty conclusions about her supposed movements.

Unfortunately, freedom and privacy were going to cost her money. She would have to get a new cell plan for herself.

The girl with the paisley backpack pushed up her sweatshirt, revealing Japanese calligraphy tattoos. She addressed Bella.

"Look Bella, it's like this. You are negotiating with a hostile nation. You can't go in and offer concessions right off the bat. You have to have a few kills under your belt. That gets their attention. It garners respect."

"Do you realize you are talking to a dog?" asked the man. He placed Bella on the ground, attached a leash to her collar, and strode away.

The door to the street opened and closed as the man left, Bella leading the way. The glass panes were clear. The lights of the city were twinkling. The empty parking lot and the abandoned gas station across the street were bathed in an eerie glow.

"You're going to go on a walk on a night like this?" asked Tinguely.

No one responded.

The door opened and closed again. The night air outside smelled like lilacs and burning plastic.

"This is the way things really are, I guess," said Tinguely. The chemicals and particulates in the air burned her eyes.

For the first time, she noticed that charred polyethylene smelled oddly of brimstone.

She suddenly could not imagine herself living here long.

****

Technology is a way of revealing.

Heidegger, *Die Technik und die Kehre* (1954)

****

THOUGHTS

Mathematical Knowledge Is Constructed:

- Thomas Hobbes (1588-1679): Mathematics and the political state both constructed from arbitrary states.

- Giambattista Vico (1668-1774): History is made by humans

in collective action.

Mathematics Is Constructed:

- Immanuel Kant (1724-1804): The mind is active in the formation of knowledge and creates categories.

- Gottlieb Fichte: The mind "posits" reality and its positing is prior even to the laws of logic.

- Hegel (1770-1831): Categories develop through time and history, focus on non-Being from Being to produce the synthesis of Becoming.

- Marx and Engels: Frameworks (or ideologies) are terms in which people understand the world; math is an ideology?

- Poincare: Mathematics is built up from mathematical induction.

- Jan E. Brouwer: Mathematics is built from the ability to count.

- Rudolf Carnap: Logical positivist—we build our idea of knowledge from sense data (logical constructions from sense data).

- Lev Vygotsky (1896-1934): Cognitive development is in stages; focuses on the social dimension of the development of a child's conceptual framework.

We thought we were so superior, didn't we – back in the twentieth century, when we sent a covey of flying men in parachute suits to the moon and back.

Men could fly. In airplanes. In helicopters. In rocketships. Or by themselves – on stage, with a wire ... someone wrote Peter Pan and a lady with a big voice enacted the part.

We broke with previous centuries. We reinvented ourselves. We "broke on through to the other side" and we went on "soma holidays."

The twentieth century represents a break from the preceding times, not only because of the emergence of globally-encompassing "total war," but also because the technologies developed during this time made human tampering with fate, human history, and nature a matter of "the touch of a button." Sweeping political change and social movements characterize the twentieth century, and they provide much of the underlying tension and motivation in the literary works of the time.

While one might imagine that the century's preoccupation with self-awareness would lead to evidence that consciousness of self was, in fact, heightened, the events of the period would argue just the converse to be true.

Case in point: the fall of the Berlin Wall and the end of Communism seemed to usher in a freedom from totalitarianism and the threat of globalized war. In retrospect, the "Cold War" seems to have been a time of remarkable calm, with a clear and unique structure that kept things at stalemate. Stalemate is good.

After all, isn't it what the Founding Fathers wanted when they looked at a bicameral system and three branches of government? Checks and balances. Stalemate. But Communism collapsed. Some countries became free. But freedom, when accompanied by corruption and chaos, is not freedom at all.

What was so great about the twentieth century? Evolutionary theory would suggest that everything evolves to become stronger, sturdier, and more likely to survive.

In contrast, the Ancient Greeks' idea of history was that the Golden Age occurred first, and everything after that was progressively worse. After Gold came Silver, and then Bronze. It's all in Hesiod's THEOGONY.

Consumerism and materialism co-opt self-consciousness by reducing spirituality itself to a commodity.

At least these were the insights of the late twentieth century.

Perhaps they were simply the self-evident truths of a planet of Peter Pans who use the promise of technology to gain power of nature in order to provoke disruption – not just in the status quo, but in processes that were, in the past, known to be inviolable law (of nature, of human nature).

I'm on a soma holiday. I'm probably not coming back. Why not? As opposed to Huxley's BRAVE NEW WORLD, a good twentieth-century classic, I'm now well into the twenty-first century. It's a harsher, more crowded place, and the technologies that were invented in the twentieth century, especially the financial instruments, are starting to break down.

The medical technologies – the genetic engineering, etc. are breaking down, too. Dolly, the cloned sheep, experienced accelerated aging and premature death.

The industrial technologies are equally problematic. Ultra-deepwater drilling experienced the wrath of Neptune. The rigs break down. Pipelines burst. Blowout preventers fail. Explosions. Spills. Death.

What technology gave, failed technology takes away – multiplied. Pynchon's entropy. Hesiod's ages: Golden, Silver, Bronze. John of Patmos's APOCALYPSE.

A planet of Peter Pans.

Dominate. No, don't dominate. This calculus is not interesting. The terms are just too diametrically opposed. Let's stay somewhere in the middle, where negotiation is at least a viable option.

"This is your recommendation?" Tinguely almost dropped the book in astonishment. She was not a prude, but it was easily the most shocking book she had ever read. And it was being proffered as high-toned reading for the teens of this small high-plains windfarm-and-slaughterhouse Texas Panhandle town.

The local Library Ladies Club had recommended *I, Vampire* for the Teen Book of the Month.

It did not seem to bother the largely Christian evangelical members of the group that the book's heroine had been made a vampire in a highly suspect, perhaps even devilish manner.

Further, these proper pillars of the community did not seem to take note that the 16-year-old protagonist of clear eyes, cherubic blonde curls, and peony lips was, in fact, part of a small army of minions—volitionless undead who skulked around in the service of the gaunt yet magnetic doppelganger of an uneasily fey, young Johnny Depp.

"That is, uh, different," said Tinguely. Her voice trailed off. "Different. Yes. I'm usually all for different, but not in this way."

"All teens feel different," said Bazila Haycroft, President-Elect of the Library Ladies Club. Bazila was a softish woman with droopy eyes and large breasts. She had a nice smile though. "*I, Vampire* shows that even if you think of yourself as a rather sickening creature with loathsome habits, you can find others who accept you."

Dead. Undead. The two states of being are too absolute for the average person to want to accept. Give me a medium or a palm reader to communicate with the part of my own consciousness I call "the spirits" or "ghosts." We love to roam the vast pasture where the very idea of the dead and the undead is as annoying as horseflies and sandburs.

"What was wrong with *I, Robot?*" asked Tinguely.

Bazila looked at her blandly.

"*I, Robot* is not so, well, sexualized. I mean, why would you want to feed teen hormones? Especially girl hormones," continued Tinguely. "Those little ladies can get pregnant, you know. Starve out that hussy madness, I say. Focus on philosophy and machines."

Tinguely had just turned 30, and had clearly forgotten what it was like to have recently weathered the storms of puberty. Or perhaps she did, and that accounted for her rather extreme position.

"I'm sorry. I don't think we've met," said Bazila, rather frostily.

"Oh. I'm Tinguely Querer. I'm just visiting. I thought I'd check out the library. Maybe make a tax-deductible donation to help you build your collection," she said, making a groping motion toward her purse. "Do you accept checks or credit cards?"

Bazila softened. It was pretty transparent that Bazila's warmth was conditional on the size of the perceived donation, but it was endearing rather than Machiavellian. "Yes, we'd love to build our literacy collection. We want to help our children."

Tinguely sighed.

"Well, I don't know why you're sinking to the level of teen vampires. Are you really so intent on destroying every single victory of feminism? You know it will happen if you encourage this nasty habit of encouraging girls to think it's exciting to be bitten, have blood drained from their necks, and then become the passionate slave of a tyrant vampire," snapped Tinguely.

"How much were you thinking of donating to our library?" asked Bazila.

****

The body: The flesh machine. Consciousness? Utterly unconscious? Programmed? Neither state is particularly satisfying. The problem resembles the free will vs. predestination dichotomy. No one wants either pure free will or absolute predestination, even though people have built religions around their favorite one in order to give it just the right level of gravitas to be convincing.

"Would you be willing to cull the girl-vampire books?" asked Tinguely. "Oh, forget it. I know you wouldn't. Plus, I'm philosophically opposed to censorship. I hate the message of the vampire books. But, I do love *I, Robot.*"

Bazila glowered.

"Tinguely, we've just met, but I want to tell you that in my opinion, *I, Robot* has all sorts of unwholesome messages, too. The machines are always on the verge of killing their masters. They are smarter, more logical, and have absolutely no conscience or feelings. The robots are sort of psychopathic, if you ask me. We think it sends the wrong message, especially to our teen boys."

Tinguely brightened at the thought of machines gaining self-awareness and either attacking their masters or simply going on strike. She looked at her iPhone. In an *I, Robot* world, her iPhone handheld device or smartphone could be her best friend. Her phone could even be her mentor. She would never have to be lonely again. Just keep the smartphone fully charged.

Truth be told, Tinguely was working on her own updated version of *I, Robot*. She gave Bazila a brief overview. She decided not to go into the parts of the book that dealt with organ harvesting and kidnapping young women to turn them into human egg incubators.

"When you finish your book, perhaps you could do a book signing here at the library," said Bazila. "And now I want to get back to *I, Vampire*."

"Bazila, I think we're just going to go around and around on this. I'm fearful of teenage sexuality. You should be, too. But you'd rather be dominated by a pale, bloodsucking undead male than a strong, consistent, and predictable machine."

"Why do we have to be dominated by anything at all?" asked Bazila.

"Because we can't be happy unless we're in distress, and we can't be happy unless we're absolutely desperate to break free from something we think is chaining our ankles and pulling us back to earth."

****

Captivity and all its synonyms. They are so potent, they almost have a taste. One could say they taste like absinthe, but that would be too easy. The spirit's captivity is the stuff of mad poets and a person who likes to extract juice from the wormwood tree.

Tinguely pulled out her checkbook and a pen.

Bazila masked her "alpha dog" dominance and feigned submission.

Tinguely laughed ruefully. "Bazila, admit it. It feels good to be a captive. It's stimulating to plot and scheme our escape. And then, there's the sweetness of the revenge fantasy. Or, if you're not in the mood to be a rebel, you can whine about your condition without doing anything."

"On behalf of the LLC, I would like to thank you most sincerely for your generous donation," said Bazila.

The donation was satisfying, but ultimately futile, thought Tinguely after she left.

Tinguely would wager all the cash she had in her wallet (which was around $350) that Bazila spent her evenings working on her own teen vampire novel. Would Bazila's version feature sexual slavery and forced abortions for stem cells?

Tinguely shuddered.

****

The taste of freedom is not sweet. It is not sour. It is either woody or metallic. Once you swallow it, you realize you've been poisoned.

"It was the best book I ever read," said the girl at the Dairy Queen, whom Tinguely spotted with a copy of *I, Vampire*. She appeared to be about 12.

"You were able to read this stuff while eating?" Tinguely was surprised. Was it the same book she had read? Were she and the girl with the book even on the same planet?

"Well, the stuff about embalming fluid was sort of creepy, but I'm not really sure what that is," said the girl. "I felt sad for Romulus. I mean, he needed blood so soooo badly."

"I think I need to be sick," said Tinguely.

"Oh. The bathroom's out of order. Don't go in. You'll be sorry," said the young girl.

"Isn't it against some sort of health ordinance to have an inoperable restroom at an eating establishment?" asked Tinguely.

"It just happened," said the girl. She picked up her book,

put it into her cute Oscar the Grouch "tween" messenger bag.

****

A state of grace is the state you're in when you realize you don't have to think about the "big issues"—life, death, or whatever it is that troubles that pesky part of the cerebral cortex that reminds you of the irreducibility of consciousness.

Flickering red lights on the horizon indicated the extent of the wind farm. The blinking red lights on the tops of the wind turbines extended to the horizon like beads on a rosary or glittering paternoster lakes seen mile high as flying over the Rocky Mountains directly northwest of here.

Human beings can't really deal with consciousness. That's why they invented religion.

It was a good night to curl up with a true crime paperback, or to watch a rerun of a beauty pageant or documentary about the secret life of the domestic house cat.

****

Angoisse/Anxiety: One can define these terms in many ways. One awkward, but revealing way is to say it's the tension one feels when one realizes they're always running the risk of being abandoned or existing in a state of revulsion—just after they've felt the glorious moment of engulfment or, well, the myth of total unity. Absolute unity is a condition reserved for the afterlife. No one really wants it in the here and now, no matter how they profess a desire for it.

The road to Wal-Mart was barricaded by police cars cordoning off the rural hospital so a medevac helicopter could land on the two-laned asphalt street leading to the emergency room. Tinguely turned the corner as a deputy sheriff waved angrily at her and a man with a headset spoke and looked at his watch.

Tinguely's stomach clenched. She averted her eyes. Her pulse raced. She did not want to think about what might happen next. She felt anxious.

As the automatic doors of Wal-Mart slid open, Tinguely felt herself calming down. The smell of grilling hotdogs mixed with disinfectant had a strangely soothing effect.

The Wal-Mart greeter said hello to Tinguely. Another offered her a glistening hunk of sausage on the end of a toothpick. When Tinguely shook her head "no" she moved on to the next guest. Tinguely did have a chance to ask the greeter if they carried Roberto Bolano's final book *2666* in Spanish. She half-expected to find it in the original Spanish, since at least 60 percent of the population spoke the language. It used to be more, but Burmese and Somalian refugees had been brought in to fill the slaughterhouse jobs that had once been filled by illegal Mexican immigrants.

At the very least, she'd be able to find the English version. She felt sure of that.

Unfortunately, it was not to be. There were no books in Spanish. There were a few Spanish language tabloids and a few DVDs featuring black and white *clásicos del cine mexicano*. She recognized Cantinflas, a populist everyman who rivaled Charlie Chaplin in popularity. Cantinflas had a bit more "chispa" or spark. At least, that was Tinguely's opinion. She had only seen one Charlie Chaplin movie, and she disagreed with its politics.

There were a few shiny bestsellers and a wall of Harlequin romances. A middle-aged woman looked up, startled, as Tinguely walked by.

Tinguely experimented with telepathy. She directed thoughts directly to the woman: "I know what you're after.

You're hooked on the raunchy hot scenes! We all know what's in those books!!"

If the woman could hear Tinguely's thoughts, she gave no indication of it. Tinguely peered into her shopping cart. A twelve-pack of Fanta Grape. An eight-pack of Charmin toilet paper. Cheerios. Doritos. Salsa. Needle-nosed pliers. Cat litter. Bunion pads.

****

The Wal-Mart book section was next to the in-store McDonald's. A young Hispanic woman sat with her two children. They were eating French fries and drinking a Coke. The woman was examining a bottle of nail polish. Tinguely thought she would enjoy *2666*. But, perhaps, she would not.

Je t'aime! It had the same sound as a meadowlark's song, or a crow, or a raven. It is the sound one makes when one is flying in one's dreams, or simply with eyes closed, gripped in a fatal embrace. (For the lonely spirit, that fatal embrace is also known as "life." For the vampire, that fatal embrace is also known as "blood.")

Back to the books. The latest vampire series was next to the section marked "Inspirational." Nowhere was there the award-winning masterwork of a thoughtful Spanish-speaking writer (translated to English), whose noir *Touch of Evil* for the twenty-first century explored what, exactly, lived in the border between states of being. Surprisingly, Bolano's work of art would focus on Ciudad Juarez and not Tijuana. In both cases, the emphasis was on appetite. At least that's what Tinguely wagered. She had no idea, but wanted to know.

If Wal-Mart could sell vampire fantasies to middle-schoolers, why couldn't they sell a novel that confronted the way people prefer to go subterranean when they feel their core identity is at risk? Why is it they go underground when self-knowledge could make them vulnerable?

Go subterranean when your core identity is compromised.

Go underground. Invest in a human trafficker. Move north, south, east, or west. Believe in reinvention.

Reinvent and wrap your fingers around the throat of hope. Touch it. Then run from it. It is the only logical way to live.

The woman seated at a bench table at McDonald's with her two children took out the nail polish, shook it, then deftly applied the tip of the tiny brush to her younger daughter's index finger. The girl was wearing a pink hoodie and wore a pink bow in her dark, wavy brown hair. Her ears were pierced. She wore pearls.

It was easier to keep the vampires in lightweight fiction written by a conservative Mormon virgin, whose creatures of the night were innocuous prom-goers and paragons of faux-Goth fashion.

****

I love you! Je'taime! Te amo! It makes no difference how one says it. The words simply reflect the inadequacy of language to express something that probably should stay ineffable. After all, if you stripped love of its ineffability, you'd probably strip it of its power.

Disappointed to not be able to buy the book, Tinguely roamed through office supplies. She decided to buy a pack of multicolored file folders and index cards. For reading material, she grabbed "The Worst Celeb Diets" issue of the *National Enquirer*. Cellulite and shots of celebrities who had packed on 50 or 60 pounds reassured her that yes, we're all ordinary mortals.

The sound of an ambulance distracted her as she walked

through the Wal-Mart parking lot. Love and death had been united since the time of Dionysus, perhaps even longer.

Death, life, and the sacred.

A north wind brought the smell of the stockyards to her. The acrid smell burned her eyes. A Burmese man wearing a long fold of cloth like a skirt walked, pushing a bicycle. A Catholic nun stood in the corner of the parking lot. A small, sandblasted, sun-faded van looked to be filled with folded lawn chairs. Tinguely saw a small box filled with plastic rosaries—the ones you'd receive as gifts at a First Communion.

Tinguely thought of the Tibetan prayer flags she had purchased in a small store near Lark Street in downtown Albany, NY. Would a refugee set up a small Buddhist shop here in the Texas Panhandle? Would the Somalis set up shop, start small enterprises here on the prairie?

Unlike the seething dynamism of the Mexican-American border, the Somalis and the Burmese were clumped together. Islands? Dollops of humanity plopped onto cracked caliche? Immiscible cultures, at least for a generation or so. That was the impression that was given.

It was a kind of protection.

At least, that is what it seemed in comparison to the cultures that did knot, twist, stream, and flow together (and apart). Helicopter rotors. A man shouting. Blood on a gurney. A man taking notes, writing. A woman searching for a book to explain it all.

And that same woman walking back to her car, forced to satisfy herself with a tabloid and the realization that the only one who had any solutions at all in the entire 10,000 square mile expanse was the lone nun with a van full of lawn furniture and rosaries.

Pray if you can.

From the Journal of TINGUELY QUERER

Air-Clipping with Zoroaster: The Sun-Magnolia Refinery

The flares from the refineries across the Arkansas River are some of the things that give Tulsa its special, creepy charm. There is nothing like the verdant riot of heavily perfuming catalpas, honeysuckles, and wild roses, mosaiced into a bizarre panorama that includes 75-year-old refinery towers, tank farms, and gas-fired power plants.

The kicker is always the presence of fire – flares burning off the natural gas that would otherwise explode. It brings to mind Baku, Azerbaijan, and Zoroastrian temples of fire, except there are no fire worshippers here in northeast Oklahoma – at least not ones who will admit it. They worship football.

COUNT. ONE, TWO, THREE. YES. NO. SEQUENTIAL ACTION, BELIEF, TIMING. WHAT DOES IT MEAN? WHAT SHOULD IT MEAN? YOU'RE NOT HERE. IT'S MY FAULT. OR PERHAPS NOT. WHATEVER IT IS, WE'RE ALL WE'VE GOT. JUST BE THANKFUL WE ARE WARM, OUR HEARTS ARE BEATING, AND LIFE FLOWS IN, OUT, THROUGH, ACROSS, AND BEHIND CONSCIOUSNESS ITSELF. PLEASE DON'T GIVE UP ON ME.

Today, all you can see on any given day are runners along Riverside Drive. They dodge the dog walkers (assorted sadists with pit bulls and Rottweilers) and the helmeted cyclists who make it an art to pass within inches of a walker or a runner's calf. I call it "air-clipping."

The cyclists love to air-clip the fat ones.

They seemed to like to air-clip me, too, but I'm not fat (at least not after I developed my tennis addiction). I'm just fun to torment. It's nothing new. I've always been some

sort of target.

COUNT, INSIDE AND OUT. BEHAVE. OR, IF YOU PREFER, DON'T BEHAVE.
YOU'RE THE ONE WITH A KEY TO MY PLACE, BUT WON'T EVER GIVE ME A
KEY TO YOUR PLACE. YOU LIKE YOUR ADVANTAGES LIKE THAT. AND, WELL,
YOU'RE THE ONE WHO PLAYED TO WIN WHILE I WAS STILL LOOKING AT
THE CEILING COUNTING CLOUDS AND DOG-SHAPED FORMS IN THE PLASTER.
MUMPS. MEASLES. CHICKEN POX. RUBELLA. IT'S WHAT EVERYONE USED
TO GET UNTIL THEY SOCIALLY ENGINEERED US TO ONLY GET THE DESIGNER
DISEASES. WE ARE OUT OF SYNC.

Just yesterday, a clutch of five or six homeless men
approached me as they made their way to an abandoned
squat house. I was pumping gas at a Phillips 66
convenience store at the corner of Utica and Cherry Street.
The pump was amazingly slow, and it took about a minute
to pump each gallon. The slow pump gave the homeless
men a chance to approach me.

Not once, but twice, even three times.

One man asked me for 35 cents. Another handed me
his business card and offered to paint my curb. Another
complimented me on the length of my legs. I was wearing
high heels. My legs weren't really as long as he thought. I
was cheating. But still, I liked the compliment and briefly
contemplated acquiescing and giving the guy the 35 cents
he said he wanted.

I paused, then I chose not to contribute. Later, I was glad.

The manager of the convenience store asked them to
please keep on their way. They did not. They simply
rounded a corner, and then, after I emerged from buying
bottled water in the convenience store, the ragtag gaggle
shuffled my way.

They needed a shot of their addiction.

I needed a shot of sympathy. Self-pity and a perverse "I'm
in the movies now" hyperrealism made me mentally role-

play scene from a DAWN OF THE DEAD zombie scene.

Where are we? What are we? What does it matter?

COUNT. COUNT WORDS. COUNT CHANGE. COUNT THE WAYS I'M JUST NOT
ABLE TO UNDERSTAND THE STARS FALLING FROM THE HEAVENS, THE SAD
INVERSIONS OF REALITY. IT'S NOT SERIOUS, OR IS IT? I DON'T KNOW. THIS
SUDDEN INABILITY TO ADD, SUBTRACT, OR COUNT HAS MADE ME WORRY.
AND YET I'M STILL ABLE TO DO ALL THE COMPLEX CALCULATIONS: HOW
MANY THREADS ARE THERE IN ONE CONVERSATION? HOW MANY TICKS
AND TOCKS IN A HICKORY CLOCK? IT'S EXACTLY 3.421 CENTIMETERS
FROM THE CORNER OF MY EYE TO THE POINT OF MY CHIN. I KNOW BECAUSE
MY TEARDROPS TOLD ME SO.

I like to think of myself as somehow different – somehow
apart from the sweaty runners and walkers. When I feel
the hackle-raising whoosh of an air-clipping at the hands
of a cyclist, and I see other runners pass me by as I wheeze
down the road, trying to lose myself in the tunes on my
iPod rather than thoughts of aging and mortality, I realize
I'm fooling myself. I'm not different.

Time is linear. Memory is not.

I run, and I measure the distance. My forward motion is
linear. My years are linear.

But still, I remember the same things, and the same sorts
of flash memories come into my mind's eye. Why is that?
The flash memories are never of anything consequential
– the scent of the flowering bush in front of the small
house my parents bought when they moved to Norman,
the rustling of bamboo around a 50s Frank Lloyd Wright-
inspired house next to a swing set and a grassy, shady
backyard along Imhoff Creek, which bordered my parent's
backyard.

My parents erected a sturdy chain-link fence the moment
they could – once they'd resolved the rather equivocal
property boundaries. Why did the bamboo-shrouded
Frank Lloyd Wright home not feel the need to barricade

away curious children and outpatients who had strayed somehow from their well-worn trail down Pickard Avenue, Hardin Drive, and Chautauqua, with the university's Bizzell Memorial Library a final destination of sorts – warm, smooth pink leather divans, bathrooms that seemed more suitable to a factory, and gargoyle-festooned towers and coppolas of the "prairie gothic" architectural wonder.

My flash memory comes with the sound of cardinals and the Spanish phrases I attached to all the birdsongs: "no quiero no quiero no quiero" or "vivir vivir vivir vivir!!!"

BABY. I CAN'T COUNT. I JUST CAN'T COUNT ANY MORE. AH YES, YOU TOLD ME YOU LOVED ME. COUNT THE WAYS, YOU SAID. COUNT THE BOUNTIFUL SOUND OF SOMETHING WE ALREADY BOUGHT, SOLD, COUNTERED. SO, ALL THAT IS LEFT IS WHAT YOUR GENERATION CLAIMED THEY WOULD NEVER LET HAPPEN. WE ARE THE HOLLOW MEN. HOLLOW. WHEN DID THAT STOP MEANING WHAT IT ALWAYS MEANT? FULSOME. EXPLOSIVE. BRANDISHING IRON. AH YES. YOU ARE WHO YOU ARE. I AM NOT. I AM FLYING UPSIDE DOWN AND IN AND OUT OF A DREAM THAT IS NEITHER MINE NOR YOUR OWN.

I live in my own country. Population 1.

Guys and girls leaving a football game. Too much tailgating. Five or six men and women piling into a trolley car. "Let's go on our Journey to Nowhere!!" Their voices are amazingly sharp and loud. Memories of having a room next to football fans after a big game. They lost. Their team's defeat only intensified the Dionysian blood-and-death dance thinly veiled as having a good time.

Surprisingly dark. Loud. Fiery. Nightmarish. When the voices are so loud you cannot distinguish syllables, much less words and sentences, what is it?

The flares case fire into the turbid waters of the Arkansas River. I cross over the entrance of a pedestrian bridge where I tripped once and skinned my elbows on concrete and railroad ties.

A mother, father, and three young children stop on the

bridge and gaze into the rapids. They are speaking in Spanish. The water is too loud, and I can't make out what they're saying. I wonder what it would be like to have a small dog.

ONE. TWO. THREE. THE ABILITY TO COUNT HAS RETURNED. I CAN. YES, I CAN. ONE, TWO, THREE. AND EVEN MORE. FOUR. FORGIVE ME, MY DEAR. FOUR, FOUR, FOUR. AND MORE.

The smell of dog food. And then, burning tar. It's a day of honeysuckle and rain.

I keep running.

Susan Smith Nash's professional career as a petroleum geologist was launched at the height of one of the many oil "boomlets" in recent times, which meant her formative years were spent coming to terms with the subsequent oil "bust" (which lasted much longer than the boom itself). The boom-bust cycles she has lived through prepared her for the labyrinthine journeys the mind takes when confronted with unexpected shifts in fortune (and one's idea of reality). It also motivated her to continue her studies in business, economics, and in English, where she earned a master's degree (emphasis in writing) and a Ph.D. Her Ph.D. focused on the use of the apocalyptic narrative by mad messiahs and doomsday cult leaders. Since that time, she has stayed connected to geology, while also bringing together her diverse backgrounds by devoting a great deal of time and energy in elearning, mlearning, and other innovative knowledge and technology transfer approaches. The desire to find connections and see the unexpected parallels and coincidences in life informs her writing, which ranges from critical essays, articles on elearning, poetry, and fiction. Her previous book, *Good Deeds Society*, received recognition in Slovenia, and was used to encourage school children to find ways to do good deeds at home, at school, and in the environment.

Made in the USA
Charleston, SC
03 May 2011